freshers

constellation edition

EM·SOLSTICE

Copyright © 2025 by Em Solstice

All rights reserved. No part of this publication may be reproduced, stored or transmitted in any form or by any means, electronic, mechanical, photocopying, recording, scanning, or otherwise without written permission from the publisher. It is illegal to copy this book, post it to a website, or distribute it by any other means without permission.

This novel is entirely a work of fiction. The names, characters and incidents portrayed in it are the work of the author's imagination. Any resemblance to actual persons, living or dead, events or localities is entirely coincidental.

First edition

ISBN 9798308360629

For T Cake,

Cause why choose right?

For Al,

Here's to all the books we've read

and all the fucks we've said

chapter one

Sweat dripped from me as I dumped the last bag in the mess of my new room. There were boxes and bags everywhere; I could barely see the surfaces underneath. Dad stood in the door frame with tears in his eyes.

"Oh Dad, come on; I'm going to be fine." I stepped over the various bags and wrapped my arms around him. There was no doubt that he was going to have a severe case of empty nest syndrome now that I was going. "You're going to be fine and I'm only an hour away on the train. I can come home every weekend if you want me to."

"No, darling, I want you to enjoy yourself. You've worked so hard to get here."

"Love you, Dad," I whispered.

"I love you too, squirt." He stroked my hair, then patted me on the head. "Do you need me to take you shopping before I head off?"

I pulled away.

"No, I'll be okay. I'll go out for a walk later and get used to the surroundings."

"More like finding the nearest chippy," he joked.

I gave him a shove. "Maybe." I stuck my tongue out at him. "Now, get out of here and give Alice a hug for me."

I walked Dad down the corridor where the doors to the three other rooms and kitchen were. The hallway was dark with only a couple of dingy light bulbs but the rooms made up for it with big windows. However, they would only open a couple of inches.

I unlocked the front door for my Dad and jumped when there was someone else on the other side about to turn their key. The guy had chestnut brown curls pushed back by one of those thin elastic headbands, dressed in a black tracksuit. Two suitcases and a plastic box were dumped behind him.

"Oh, hi, sorry." I blushed.

"Not a problem." He held out his hand to me and I carefully shook it. "The name is Eli."

"Daphne," I answered.

My Dad cleared his throat and the guy looked up, straightening himself and holding his hand out to him. Dad gripped his hand so tightly I could see it turn white.

"Eli." He squeezed out, trying not to show that it hurt.

"Nice to meet you, Eli. I'm John and I hope you'll look after my daughter."

"Of course, Sir. It will be my pleasure."

Dad let go of his hand and Eli cradled it as the blood circulation restarted. My Dad turned towards me.

"Maybe I should stay a little longer." In the corner of his eye, he glanced at my new flatmate.

"Dad. I'll be fine. Besides, it's a long enough drive as it is. I'll call you later. Promise." I was sure that if he didn't leave soon, he wouldn't go at all. I had known I was going to be living with three boys but it wasn't information that I shared with him. I wouldn't have been staying in flat 55 if he had known; I'd be dragged down to the office in seconds and he would have demanded I be moved.

"I'll call you when I stop at the services." He kissed the top of my head.

My cheeks blushed as I glanced at Eli; the last thing I needed was him teasing me for being a 'daddy's girl'.

"Okay, bye. Love you," I said, grabbing his arms and shoving him past Eli.

Dad stepped over the doorway and carried on walking but looked over his shoulder several times before he disappeared around the corner to the lift. I sighed. I loved my Dad, how could I not when it was just us? But sometimes there was nothing more suffocating than when he tried to play both mother and father.

Then I looked at the gorgeous guy leaning against the wall in the hallway beside his belongings. It was at that moment I remembered how sweaty and gross that I was.

"Well... your Dad seems really...chill."

I raised an eyebrow at him and laughed. Our eyes locked for a split moment; I quickly looked away and chewed on my lip.

"Anything but chill. I guess I should go and unpack." I turned my heel, heading back to my room. Eli was undeniably hot and I was to be in hot water all year if the other two were anything like him.

I kicked the bags in the way so my door was able to shut, then pressed my back against it, taking a deep breath. The silence was deafening, my ears were ringing. Miles away from home in a city that I didn't know, without parental supervision for the first time in my life. How much was I going to miss my Dad when it had only been the two of us for so long? And how the hell was I going to fit everything in my room?

My eyes trailed over how mess it was already; there was no doubt it was going to take me hours to sort out.

On my left was the door leading to the small en-suite and then further down on the left was a wardrobe facing the opposite wall, creating a tight hallway, then a double bed. It was also the wall where my window was; the large pane was almost floor to ceiling. The rest of the small area was taken up by a corner desk that would be covered in my make-up within a week. My walls were a boring magnolia, cursed to get marks on them and lose my deposit.

I spent almost two hours trying to fit all of my belongings into one room. When I was finally finished, I threw myself onto the bed, sinking into my new duvet and pillows. The smell of BO was overpowering and I was in desperate need of a shower. But before I could step into the cubicle my phone rang, disturbing my peace.

After twenty minutes on the phone with my dad while he had his midway coffee, I showered, soaking my hair in a hair mask and shaving my legs.

I was drying off when there was a knock at my room. Wrapping my towel around myself tightly, I turned the lock. I hid my body behind the door and poked my head out, doing a double take when I saw a guy in front of me. I'd expected Eli to be on the other side but it was some new entirely.

His dirty blonde hair was pushed away from his face with a backwards cap but I could see reluctant strands poking out the front. He had thick, trimmed eyebrows that complimented his blue eyes and sharp jawline, dressed in a tight white t-shirt and a pair of grey jogging bottoms. I was in awe and completely fucked. The last thing I needed was another incredibly hot male room mate offering boyish smiles all year round.

"Hey, I thought I'd come and introduce myself; my name's Nate."

"Daphne. I'd shake your hand but I'm kind of not dressed right now."

A small smirk danced across his lips.

"Me and Eli were going to head out later, find a shop, if you want to come with us?"

"Umm, yeah, sure." I smiled. "Can you give me like an hour?"

"Take your time, sweetheart."

My cheeks turned red and I could feel the heat on my skin.

"Okay, I'll be out soon," I mumbled and shut the door. "What the fuck," I whispered afterwards to myself. I repeated it over and over again as I got ready.

As I was about to leave my room, I turned back and decided to add a little make-up to my face, considering both guys had seen me in one of my rougher states already. I tried to tame my long brown hair into a claw clip and questioned why I hadn't cut it short like I had planned to.

Dressed and armed in a pair of my favourite black leggings and fluffy brown teddy bear fleece jumper, I took a deep breath and made my way down the hallway where I could hear voices in the kitchen.

The kitchen and living room area was the biggest part of the flat, split down the middle by the breakfast bar. The kitchen was the cheapest thing they could find and I could tell that by the strange wood effect vinyl they had stuck to the doors which was peeling off at the corners. I unlocked my phone and took a picture because there was no way I was going to lose my deposit over something we hadn't even done.

The sound of my camera caught the attention of Nate, Eli and another guy standing by the sofas. My final roommate had light brown hair with natural blond flecks. He stared at me with bold jade green eyes, his full lips curving into a smile as I stepped closer and held out my hand.

"Hi, I'm Daphne." I smiled and nodded at him.

"Aiden." He took my hand and gently shook it.

"Are you coming shopping with us?" I asked.

"Yeah, don't think I'll unpack until tomorrow," he replied and dropped my hand.

"You guys ready?" I asked. All three said yes and Nate pulled out his phone.

"We're probably gonna need this, though." He showed maps on his screen.

The four of us walked together, following Nate's map to the big Tesco which was a mile and a half away from our building. It was mostly through streets that were no doubt home to other students. Then we reached a dark cycling path with scattered lighting; I wrapped my arms around myself, looking over into the dark bushes. The sun had set now and I wouldn't be surprised if we came across some wildlife.

"You okay?" Aiden nudged me.

I looked up at him and nodded.

"I'm okay, just taking in the surroundings," I answered. Nate and Eli were talking slightly ahead of us.

While we had walked, there had been small talk getting to know one another. I'd learned that Nate was studying sports medicine, Eli was studying music and Aiden was studying business. The three of them had told me how much literature suited me when I told them my own subject.

I squealed as I slipped on a patch of mud on the path. Aiden's arms flew out to catch me before I landed on my ass. I clung onto his forearms as I steadied myself. Nate and Eli stopped and turned around to check on me.

"Are you okay?" Nate asked.

"What happened?" Eli stepped towards me and touched my arm.

"I just slipped," I answered. "I'm okay." I smiled, tucking a piece of hair behind my ear.

"Maybe we should get an Uber back home," Aiden suggested, "before Daphne ends up on her ass."

I smacked him on the arm playfully and Aiden carefully manoeuvred so that we were holding hands side by side, our fingers intertwined as we resumed walking . His hand clasped mine so tightly as if Aiden was afraid I was going to fall again. The familiar heat bloomed on my cheeks and I was thankful for the cover of darkness.

"Yeah, I don't think I have the energy to walk back," Eli called over his shoulder.

Only a few minutes later, we exited the dark path and came out by the side of Tesco Extra. It was pretty quiet for 9pm on a Saturday night. Nate grabbed the trolley we passed in the car park and we walked towards the entrance. I let go of Aiden's hand and it was almost like he refused to drop mine for a moment.

I had told myself that I couldn't get involved with flatmates, else it would only end up in tears. I caught up with Nate, creating some distance between Aiden and I.

The fluorescent lighting was blinding compared to the night sky. It took us a lot longer than it should have to gather basics; we'd decided that this weekend it would be nice if we all ate together before classes made it impossible. On our way to the check-out, we walked down the hair-care aisle. I stopped looking at the line of hair dyes relatively quickly, my eyes drawn to the midnight black.

Something new, something different; a fresh start for the next three years of my life. I picked up three boxes and caught up with the boys. The shopping had been split into four sections already and I dumped the addition into my section which included a bar of Galaxy cookie crumble.

"Hair dye?" Eli asked curiously.

"Isn't that what university is all about, trying things that you would have never have thought of before? " I shrugged.

We paid for our shopping and waited outside for our Uber. It was even colder than before and standing still wasn't helping at all. I wrapped my arms around myself and hid my hands in the sleeves of my jumper, trying to keep warm. Fabric was laid over my shoulders and I noticed that Eli had given up his jacket for me.

"You're going to get cold," I said, trying to take it off. Eli planted two hands on my shoulders.

"Leave it; it's only for a few minutes."

"Thank you." I smiled at him and pulled the jacket closer around my shoulders, smelling his strong aftershave.

It was only two minutes later that our Uber pulled up. Nate and Aiden put the shopping in the boot of the car while I buckled myself into the middle seat. Eli sat on my left and Nate climbed in next to me on the right; I was wedged between two gorgeous guys. Aiden got into the front and glanced before him, as if he was checking up on me. His eyes lingered longer than I expected with a spark of jealousy that he wasn't crammed next to me.

No one knew what to say while the Uber driver took us home; Aiden attempted to make small talk with him but it soon died out. We were all happy when he pulled up outside our building. Eli got out and then held out his hand to help me. I accepted his offer, using my other hand to hold his jacket on my shoulders.

I picked up one of the bags from the curb and took my fob from my pocket. I waited, holding the door open for the three guys as they got the other few bags. Once we were back in our flat, we dumped them on the kitchen side. Eli and Aiden began to put everything away while Nate passed me the boxes of dye.

"Do you want some help? I used to help my Mom," he offered.

"Yeah, I'd appreciate that. Let me just go put on an old t-shirt and we can sit in here."

I got changed quickly and walked back into the kitchen. Everything had been put away and Nate was sitting on the sofa, legs open, shaking a bottle of hair dye. Aiden sat at one of the breakfast stools while Eli sat on the counter with a beer in his hand. I made my way over to Nate and he nodded between his legs. I blushed slightly but sat down anyway, passing him my brush and hair clip and turning my head towards the other two guys.

Nate took his time putting the dye in my hair, making sure that he covered every strand. The four of us talked, getting to know each other more and more. After he added all the dye to my hair, Nate dug his glove-covered fingers into my scalp and massaged it in. I threw my head back and moaned.

"Mmmm, that feels good."

All eyes were on me as my cheeks blushed the darkest pink possible on my pale skin. I cleared my throat and stood up.

"I'll be back when it's done." Then I scurried off to my room, embarrassed that Nate's fingers had made me react like that.

I should have got myself rehoused as soon as I found out that I was going to be the only girl stuck with three guys. I only had myself to blame if it blew up in my face.

chapter two

I sang along to 'What About Us' by Pink as I tied up my trainers. I was 48 hours into my fresh start at uni. Last night, we had gone on our first night out and my head was still throbbing and my throat drier than the Sahara Desert. It had just been the four of us last night; no one had really got to know anyone else yet. I enjoyed our little bubble already; I knew it was probably the honeymoon period and before I knew it, we would be at each other's throats because someone hadn't done the washing up.

Reaching over to pick up my tote bag, I slid my keys into it. I yawned and held my head back wincing. When I walked out into the hallway, all three guys were waiting for me.

"I feel rough," I grumbled.

"Took your time, didn't you?" Eli teased.

"You try bringing yourself from the brink of death." I gave him a little shove.

In return, Eli grabbed me from behind and spun me in the tight space.

"Put me down! I'm gonna puke!" I cried, flailing my legs. Eli answered my pleas and Nate leaned over to ruffle my freshly dyed black hair. I caught his wrist before he could. "Don't you dare; you'd need to sleep with one eye open." My attempt to be terrifying was failing because I was shorter than all of them.

"Try your best, sweetheart." He smirked.

I let go of his wrist and Aiden pulled open the front door. I stepped through first and waited in the small hallway. On each floor there were two flats. Opposite us was a group of girls that I hadn't seen much of in the past couple of weeks, only hearing the loud music and the giggling when they came home. I suspected my situation was envied because the girls were all smiles and fluttering lashes when they saw any three of the boys. But then, when I appeared, they would disappear with one final look up and down of me. As if I were to blame for the housing arrangements.

The boys walked out of the flat and Aiden locked the door, taking his role of leader very seriously. It had happened naturally in the dynamic of the four of us. He was probably the only reason that security hadn't got us rehoused the other night because of the flat party, one of many they had decided to fill our weekends with.

We headed down in the lift and left the building. It was almost a half an hour walk to campus but the walk took you through the local park with pretty scenery and tons of squirrels running about. Various small groups were heading the same way, people that you wouldn't necessarily put together which meant they were also groups of housemates who hadn't made any friends outside of their bubble yet.

When we got to the main hall, the place was heaving, students packed together like sardines. Almost every stall had its own set of speakers that, from a distance, all merged together, nearly drowning out the sound of students.

"Anything in particular you guys wanted to check out?" Aiden asked.

"I was gonna look at the societies," I said. "God knows where they are in this mess, though."

"Come on, I'll come with you." Eli wrapped his arm around my shoulder.

"I'm going to check out the events this week," Nate spoke, then turned towards Aiden. "Coming with, bro?"

Aiden nodded.

"Yeah, why not? Catch you guys in a bit. Text us on the group chat if you need us," he spoke, then he walked off into the crowd with Nate.

The societies were shoved at the back of the hall to make room for the sponsorships of the fresher's fair, junk food and alcohol mainly. It was also a quieter part of the hall. Eli stopped to talk to someone who was part of some music society and I wandered further down the line of options until I came to the 'Open Mic' society.

Two people were sitting behind the table, one girl with long black curly hair and dark brown eyes. Her outfit screamed that she had just walked out of a private school; a crisp white blouse and brown tartan skirt. She gave me a big smile and picked up a flyer.

"Are you interested in joining?" she asked, handing me it. There was an outline of a school microphone on a stand with a red background, then all the information printed below it.

"I'm a little shy about performing anything but I'd love to come and check it out," I told her.

"We perform every month. We've started to bring in most of the crowd with our work." The guy stood up. The way he spoke gave me the impression he thought very highly of himself which was even more off putting when open mics were about expressing yourself.

"Wow; that sounds amazing." I smiled politely. "Well thank you. I'll come along to the next event." I turned back around to try and spot Eli in the crowd.

"They're a lot, aren't they?" Someone spoke directly into my ear and I jumped, looking over my shoulder. The girl standing behind me had straight bright ginger hair and was wearing a pair of jeans and a long-sleeved bodysuit that hugged her curves. I recognised her from my induction, she was in most of the same classes as me. "Hi, I'm Madison." She grinned and held out her hand.

"Daphne. And yeah, they're a lot," I agreed, shaking her hand. "We're in the same classes, aren't we? You're studying English and Creative Writing too?"

"That's the one. I'm pretty sure I've seen you around the Liberty block as well? I'm on the third floor."

"Yeah, I'm on the fifth."

"I guess that means we've got to be friends then, doesn't it?" she teased.

"Fancy grabbing a drink later in the Union?" I asked. Madison seemed chill enough that we could be friends and having someone other than the guys was great.

"Or maybe we can all get wasted tonight at our flat party?" Eli stepped in front of us. "Eli, flat 55." He held out his hand to her.

"Madison but call me Madi; flat 51. So, you guys must be the reason we've had security scouting around the building last night."

"They said we made too much noise but personally I don't think any of us sleep at night anyway, isn't that the student thing to do?" Eli smirked.

"So, we decided on another flat party then?" I asked.

"Yeah, cheaper; we have tons of booze left over from pres the other night."

"I'd love to come and see what all the fuss is about," Madison replied.

"Great, come over whenever, I'm sure you girlies have all that getting ready shit to do." Eli was lucky that I liked Madison so far, else I would have kicked him in the nuts.

"Oh please, you spend more time on your hair then I do." I rolled my eyes.

chapter three

"One, two, three, go!" Eli called out. We lifted our shot glass and the harsh taste of the cheap Sourz ran down the back of our throats. I pulled a face and put my cheap, plastic shot cup on our kitchen counter.

"That shit is vile; I'd rather drink tequila." I shook my head, the aftertaste of Sourz leaving a sickly sweet taste in my mouth.

Nate picked up the bottle and filled my shot cup again, the bright red liquid staring at me.

"Not again," I groaned, flicking my hair off my shoulder.

"Come on and then we'll get a taxi." He nudged me.

"Where is Madison, I need her," I fake cried. Aiden chuckled at me and Eli put his arm around my shoulder. All my flatmates were dressed in their best and classic clothing, jeans and plain t-shirts. Their hair was perfectly styled and faces shaved, apart from Aiden who had left stubble on his face.

"Probably still curling her hair or some other girly shit," Nate shrugged. "Bottoms up."

I lifted the cup to my mouth and downed the cherry acid again, stepping back and shaking my head.

"Okay, no more," I said. "I'm gonna get Madison and we can go." I coughed before sliding off the stool and got my bag off the counter.

"We'll see you downstairs," Aiden laughed.

I waved as I exited the kitchen and walked out the front door. I decided on using the stairs rather than the lift, rushing down in my chunky black boots; the lift was old and slow which would have only wasted time. I'd already learned my lesson that skinny heels were a bad idea and you ended up tripping up and face planting the floor. At the bottom of the stairs, I pulled down my dress to cover my ass properly.

The door to Madison's flat was already in the latch, allowing me to let myself in. The layout of the flat was an exact copy of mine upstairs; a long corridor of four rooms and the kitchen on the right as you walked in. Their kitchen door was propped open with a flimsy door stop, meaning her flatmates had a clear view of me letting myself in. I offered an awkward smile and carried on down the hall to Madison's room. Her door had been left open too so I strolled in, using my foot to open it. Her music was on low, some drum and bass track that I hadn't heard.

The lighting was dim, the big light was off and her room was illuminated by her large salt lamp and fairy lights. Madison was laying back on her bed with a glass of wine on her bedside table. She was scrolling through her phone and I nudged her foot.

Madison glanced over at me, smiling and dropping her phone.

"Hi babes, are we going?" she asked, sitting up.

"The boys are going to meet us downstairs." I held my head out to her. "Please, don't run off tonight," I jokingly added.

Madison took my hand and rolled her eyes, letting me pull her up and then taking one last swig of her wine from her bedside table.

"I'm not going to get lost."

"You always get lost and I have to find you," I told her as she grabbed her bag. "Do you know how many times I've had to find you over the past two weeks?"

"Okay, you have a point but I won't this time. I promise." Madison pinched my cheek and I swatted her away.

We walked out of her flat and down the stairs where the boys were waiting outside, huddled together. Eli was smoking, one hand in his pocket, while Nate had his hands in her jacket and Aiden was looking down at his phone. I pressed the button on the wall and we pushed open the door together. The boys looked over, smiles dancing on their lips.

"Taxi is on the way," Aiden spoke. I wrapped my arms around myself, protecting myself from the breeze.

"How long?" I asked.

"It says it's three minutes away."

"Oh my god!"

I jumped at the chalkboard voice that I was far too familiar with. The three girls that lived opposite us made their way across from the smoking shelter.

"Are you going out tonight too?"

I watched as Olivia, the tall brunette, threw her arm around Eli, making my skin crawl.

I hadn't taken a liking to our neighbours. The three of them had been friends a long time and somehow had managed to get themselves into the same flat. They'd started to invite themselves in any chance they'd get, just to hang off Eli, Nate and Aiden. The last thing that I wanted was for them to join us on *our* night out.

"Yeah, we're headed to Walkabout," Nate smiled at them and I wanted to kick him in the balls for telling them where we were going. Why would he do that, knowing full well they were going to follow us?

"Us too!" Elisha, another of the girls replied, overly preppy which made me want to gag. I looked at Madison who had turned to me. We were on the same page and didn't need to confirm it. I'd disappear with Madison if it meant getting away from flat 54.

"Oh, nice," Eli grinned. Another one that I wanted to kick in the balls and it must have been written all over my face. Aiden was looking right at me, head tilted in curiosity, itching not to smile at the jealousy written all over my face.

It wasn't like I wanted them all to myself; I just happened to not like the girls very much. But I liked our bubble, the way we were. We'd all started to make friends but I was determined to not let my flat become one of those that were a bunch of strangers.

Madison stepped closer to me for warmth and I lay my head against hers. Elisha, Olivia, and Beth stepped closer to us. She stepped closer to Eli and held her hand out.

"Twos?" she asked. Eli reluctantly passed off the last part of his cigarettes just as a pair of headlights entered the car park.

"I guess that's for us," I said, grabbing Madison's hand and hobbling towards the black cab. I pulled open the door and smiled at the driver.

"For Aiden?" I asked.

"That's the one," the driver replied. I stepped up into the cab and threw myself down on the furthest seat in the back. Madison sat next to me and it was only moments later that my three flatmates joined us, Nate sitting beside Madison, while Eli and Aiden took the fold-down seats. As soon as the door was shut, the driver pulled off.

Like most nights, the club we had chosen was packed with students who shouldn't be spending their maintenance loan on cheap alcohol that they'll be throwing up on the street in a few hours. The streets were clean at least for now, the pathways filled with students dressed in tight clothing or their best jeans. Uber drivers pressed down on their horns to scare off students who were standing in the road and the smell of Kebabs were already in the air waiting for the flood of customers later on.

Our group had found a small space to stand with a ledge to place our drinks. We just had enough room to dance as the club played old school mcfly for their 2000s night. Madison and I were screaming the lyrics in each other's faces, shaking our hair, completely intoxicated by our sixth drink.

The buzz of alcohol danced on my skin and urged me to be free and happy. I lost my footing and almost fell into Madison. We locked eyes with one another and laughed. I leant back into Aiden who was standing behind me. The song ended and Madison leaned over to shout into my ear:

"Toilet break!"

I nodded.

"We're going to the toilet! We'll be back," I called over the music to the boys and they tilted their heads in understanding.

"Be careful," Aiden warned me.

We held hands as we made our way to the toilets in the back of Walkabout. My ears were numb when we were finally away from the music and in the quiet toilet area. The bathroom was already a mess: empty glasses and toilet paper on the floor, along with water pooling across the tiles. There were a few pairs of girls in the toilet and by the mirrors were Olivia, Elisha and Beth, who clearly hadn't spotted us.

"If she hadn't been there earlier, they would have just stayed with us tonight," Olivia rolled her eyes, except they finally locked with mine.

I folded my arms and raised my brow at her. I was too intoxicated to keep my mouth shut but I'd always promised that I wouldn't start fights, only finish them, just like Disney had taught me. That, and I don't think I was sober enough for my slap to land correctly. Bitching about another girl was petty and especially because of a guy, or guys, in their case.

She didn't falter, only smirked at me. Madison grabbed my arm, knowing that I was ready to blow.

"Something to say?" I called over.

"Only that you're a slut," Olivia shrugged.

I closed my eyes for a second, biting down on my lip, trying to think of reasons not to bitch slap her into next week and I couldn't find a single one. I managed to tear myself out of Madison's grip and head straight for Olivia.

But she was one step ahead of me. The drink she was holding ended up all over me, my hair and face covered in cheap sticky cola and what smelled like vodka. I had the urge to gag due to my drunken state. I was frozen in my spot. Elisha and Beth even had a stunned look on their faces as their leader's mouth turned up into a Cheshire Cat smirk.

"You know jealousy isn't a good look on you," I told her, wiping the alcohol from under my eyes.

"Well, no one will go near you looking like a wet dog." She stepped closer to me and I clenched my fists as the eyes around the bathroom were all on us.

"I don't get what your problem is. I didn't choose where I got placed but get the picture because Aiden, Eli and Nate don't fucking want you. There's been countless opportunities for them to shag you and it hasn't happened. Get over it."

I felt Madison tug on my arm again.

"Come on, they aren't worth it. Let's go home before I kill a bitch." Madison glared.

Madison pulled me away, our hands linked as we pressed ourselves against the wall and headed for the exit. I could feel the cola drying on my skin and the smell of alcohol up my nose. It was starting to make me feel sick and it only got worse when we stepped outside when my alcohol intake hit me.

I let go of Madison's hand and pushed back my sticky hair, keeping my breathing as level as possible. I looked over to my friend who had pulled out her phone and ordered a taxi home.

"I need to tell the boys," I told her.

"I'll text them. You just stand there and breathe before you go back in there and bitch slap Olivia up," she joked.

I nodded and looked up at the night sky; the air and alcohol was hitting me like a ton of bricks, piling on top of my anger. I squeezed my eyes shut, trying to stop myself from throwing up but the nausea overtook me.

I dipped towards the wall beside the club, placing my hands on the wall and throwing up the contents of my stomach, the smell only making me retch all over again. Madison's hand rubbed my back gently.

"I got you; get it up."

"I haven't even drunk that much," I groaned. "But the smell of flat vodka and coke is vile." I gasped as I heaved again at the thought and only bile spilled out. I spat out the salvia in my mouth and stood up straight, pressing my back against the wall.

"You good?" Madison asked, pulling her hair bobble from her long ginger hair and giving it to me instead.

"Thanks and yeah. I just want to shower and get this shit off me," I said, pulling my hair up into the worst messy bun I could have done. "What the fuck, man," I sighed, remembering earlier.

"I know, they're insane."

"How the hell am I the slut? I'm not the one throwing myself over a bunch of guys every moment I land my eyes on them." I took a deep breath, still feeling slightly queasy.

"We both know you're not. Let them be jealous bitches; just like you said, it's not like you got to pick who you were housed with." Madison stood next to me, avoiding the puddle of vomit where many had hurled before.

And exactly where I gagged again one minute later.

chapter four

I covered my ears at the sound of the sudden bass blasting from Eli's new speakers. He scrambled to turn the volume down and turned to look at me.

"Sorry, Daph." He smirked.

"You know those things are going to get us a strike right? They literally shake the walls."

Our flat had gained a reputation over the past few weeks and we had become security's arch nemesis for breaking the rules, especially since Nate rubbed his ass against the office window at the end of fresher's week.

"Live a little," Aiden whispered down my ear, startling me. He was dressed in a clean white t-shirt and a pair of black jeans. His hair was textured and swooped across his forehead, he'd even plucked his eyebrows which had surprised me.

"Yeah, living on the streets when we get kicked out." I strutted past him to return to my room.

Listening to my playlist of throwback classics, which included No Regrets by Dappy, I straightened my hair for extra length and applied a heavy layer of make-up which included filling in the bald spot in my brow. I threw on a pair of washed-out blue jeans and a long sleeved white bodysuit that wasn't going to last the night.

There was loud thumping on my door and I pulled myself up off the floor to answer it. I opened my door and turned to grab my trainers off my bed. Nate strolled in wearing a pair of dark blue jeans and a black crewneck. The strong smell of his aftershave filled my room and overtook the perfume I had sprayed earlier. Nate wolf whistled and winked at me.

"You know that catcalling girls is classed as harassment these days?" I raised my eyebrow at him.

"I can't help it, Daph. You're just too stunning for your own good, you know?"

"What do you want? Have you run out of rice again?" I teased. Nate, being the Gym buff that he was, went through so much rice and was constantly using everyone else's.

"No, I was just checking you out," he smiled. I felt my cheeks burn red. I reminded myself that Nate was only joking and that you should shit where you eat, as they say. That nothing good could ever come out of falling into bed with one of your flatmates.

At least I knew that Nate was only teasing; he was flirty, playful and, even on my most miserable days, he managed to make me smile.

"How about you go check out the girls you actually have a chance with?" I jabbed.

"Ouch, you wound me." He pressed his hand over his heart dramatically .

"Come on, I need a drink." I crossed Nate in the small strip of my room. My boobs grazed his chest. I looked up and for a moment I considered it. It wouldn't have been hard to reach onto my tip toes and kiss him. I smiled instead and brushed past him to the door.

Nate followed me closely and locked the door behind me. I didn't want some random drunk students using my room to screw each other. I passed Nate my key and he rolled his eyes. One thing we had learned was that I was a nightmare for locking my door and forgetting where I had 'safely' put my key at the end of the night.

I pushed open the kitchen door and used the broken microwave to prop it open.

The main lights were off and you could hear the whirling of the old 2000s disco ball that Eli had found in the charity shop down the road. It was placed in the centre of the breakfast bar where my red-headed best friend was sitting on my counter talking to Eli and Aiden. I squealed when I saw her and basically jumped on her.

"Please never visit home again," I mumbled.

"That's very tempting. Mom was a nightmare," she groaned and I took the stool next to her.

"Makes me happy that mine decided to poof into thin air," I joked.

"I'm already on my third Aiden cocktail and I bumped into the bitches next door on my way." Madison scrunched her nose up and lifted her glass to take a sip.

I looked over to Aiden who was leaning against the counter. He poured me a glass of something bright green and handed it to me.

"Okay, I don't think I want to try this anymore," I laughed.

"It won't kill you," Aiden told me, popping a straw into my glass. "At least, I don't think it will."

"Not sure about that; those things are strong as fuck." Eli shook his head.

"It's fine, drink." Madison forced the glass to my lips, spilling some of the mixture down my cleavage. It tasted nice but it burned my throat like I imagined acid would.

"Madi!" I exclaimed, laughing and pushing the glass away. I wiped away the sticky substance between my boobs.

"You can't even tell and besides, the light is off anyway." My best friend was definitely already well on her way to being smashed.

There was no chance I was catching up and I had tried. Four hours in and Madsoni was still ahead of me but we were both dancing on the breakfast counter. Eli had moved his precious disco lights out of harm's way when I'd nearly knocked them off. The entire flat kitchen was packed full of students from our building, the walls rattling with the intensity of the speakers.

Aiden was close by, his arms ready to catch me. He was terrified that I was going to fall and had tried to pull me down several times. Aiden was taking his role of protector and leader of our flat seriously.

I loved the way we had all fallen into our own positions. Aiden was the leader, Eli was the one who made us laugh, Nate was our chef and nutritionist, and me? I was the voice of reason when they were too hungover to go to uni.

My foot slipped on a spilt drink on the counter and I almost lost my balance. Aiden grabbed my waist and he pulled me down, not taking no for an answer. I squealed. He placed me safely on my feet and I looked up at him. Under the multi-coloured lights, I couldn't make out his green eyes which disappointed me. I smiled up at him and I knew for a fact that I looked completely smashed.

'Tik Tok' by Kesha began to play and I sang at him, stepping up onto my tip toes and pressing my forehead against his. Aiden pulled away from me.

"Oh, come on," I complained.

"You need to go to bed," he shouted over the music.

"It's barely one." I laughed, grabbing his hands and forcing him to dance with me.

"And I'm the one who is gonna have to hear you complain about your hangover tomorrow. We both know you're about to crash." It was Aiden all over; he knew me better than I knew myself. My feet had started to hurt an hour ago.

"Gonna tuck me in, Dad?" I rolled my eyes.

"No but I will." Eli spoke into my ear, lifting me up and spinning me around. I screamed as we bumped into a few people. He put me back down on my feet and nuzzled into my neck. "I'm so sleepy," he mumbled against my neck. I was surprised I could hear him. Then, just when I wanted to prove I didn't need putting to bed like a toddler, I yawned.

Aiden smirked as he raised his drink to his lips.

"Nate has my door key," I told Eli.

"I'll grab it for you. I think he's making out with some girl in his room."

I nodded and unwrapped myself from Eli. My stomach was churning at the alcohol contents in my body or the thought of Nate kissing a girl, although I couldn't figure out which.

I kissed Aiden's cheek and looked to see Madison sitting with her legs crossed on the counter talking to some guy. I'd text her good night, I decided.

I walked out the room and followed the hall down to the bottom where my door was. I leaned against it as Eli let himself into Nate's room. He came back out seconds later, laughing and walking down to me, dangling my key in the air.

He unlocked my door and I stumbled in, throwing myself on my bed. I moaned when the light was turned on right above me and covered my eyes with my arm.

"Eli. What the fuck?" I snapped.

"I'm trying to find your PJs."

I sat up and looked at him routing through the clothes pile.

"Just give me your shirt," I shrugged. "I want my bed."

Eli pulled his shirt off and chucked it at me.

I stood, wobbled, and unbuttoned my jeans. "Turn," I ordered.

Eli turned and faced the wall as I struggled to strip down. My jeans were too tight and took me longer than it should have to peel them off. I sighed as I finally dumped them on the floor and popped the buttons on my bodysuit. I pulled it over my head and slipped on his shirt. I wrapped my arms around myself, drawing the fabric in close, each inch smelling of his aftershave as if he were pressed against me.

"You're good," I called, climbing under my duvet. I flinched at the cold sheets, a shiver running through my body. Eli climbed onto the bed, kicking his shoes to the floor.

He then turned on my TV and grabbed some random snacks from my bedside table. We cuddled up watching reruns of Family Guy, mindless TV, while we both sobered up. Eli filled up the glass of water we were sharing multiple times. The headache had started to set in and there was no way of escaping it.

"My head is killing me," I whined, resting my head on his shoulder, my arm thrown lazily around his middle. Eli smelled like Sauvage and you wouldn't think it was fake but I'd seen the bottle that came in the post from one of those dupe sites. When you're a student, you don't get the luxuries of a nearly £100 aftershave.

But it didn't matter. Either way, Eli was like a comfort blanket; I'd fallen asleep on him countless times when we had watched movies in the past.

"You know what they say gets rid of a headache?" he mumbled. I could tell his eyes were closed; he was going to fall asleep any minute.

"What?" I replied.

"Orgasms."

My breath hitched and I lifted my head to look at him. I was waiting for the other foot to drop, for us to burst out laughing. Only he didn't. Eli opened his eyes and looked at me. We were staring at one another for what felt like forever, only now and again I lowered my eyes to look at his lips.

"Did you really just say that?" I whispered.

"I think so. I don't think I'm entirely sober."

"Is that your excuse?"

"I don't think I need an excuse to do this," he whispered. He bent down to close the gap between us and I sucked in a breath as our lips touched. It was the breaking of the floodgates. I'd spent weeks ignoring that pull between me and the boys. Eli had been the winner, the one to take the step between the four of us. I lifted my hand to touch his cheek, pulling him in closer because I was afraid he was going to pull away from me. His hand ran down my arm and onto my waist, stopping at the hem of the shirt. He pulled away and the silence was deafening. His sea-glass blue eyes twinkled and he smiled at me.

I nodded my head slightly and it was all he needed to slip past the fabric, his forefinger dancing along the hem of my underwear. He leaned in to kiss me again, just a peck on the corner of my mouth as his hand slipped into the shirt. My heart was racing as I moved the position of my legs to give him better access. There was no doubt that I wasn't 100 percent sober and there would be regrets in the morning. But I couldn't form a "stop" on my lips because it was the last thing I wanted him to do.

His fingers grazed over me; they were cold to the touch and I could feel the heat pulsing from me. I pushed my hips forward, nudging him to take it further. When his fingers finally made contact with my clit, I closed my eyes in bliss. While Eli was the wrong choice, flatmates were always the wrong choice, I swore to myself that I was going to enjoy every second of it.

He placed two fingers on my clit and rubbed gently in a circular motion while looking me dead in the eye, his mouth twisted up into a smirk.

"I've thought about worshipping this body so many times. Almost every morning, I imagine that my hand is your mouth or...this pretty tight hole." With one simple movement, his two fingers slipped inside of me and I gasped. My hand wrapped around the back of his neck and my nails slightly dug in. I was already fairly soaked, getting wetter by the second. Torturously slow, he pumped his fingers in and out. "Gonna let me help you with that headache of yours?"

I nodded, utterly speechless.

Eli ripped the duvet off my body and pulled me down the bed, lifting my knees up and prising them apart so I was laid out before him like a meal. He smirked at me as he used his hands to snap the thin string of my cheap Primark thong. I was bare to him and his eyes lit up as he lowered himself to my pussy.

The second he ran his tongue over my slit, I moaned. I was grateful that the party was still going on; no one would hear when Eli made me scream. He was bent over, face in my pussy. His tongue flicked over my clit and I whimpered, the small knot in my stomach waking up. His tongue dipped into my hole. I bit down on my lip, closing my eyes, taking in every nerve he set alight. Eli replaced his tongue with his two fingers, deep down to the knuckle and curling them in the spot that had me almost withering. His lips latched gently onto my clit as he thrust his fingers inside of me.

I could have died and gone to heaven.

I wrapped my fingers in Eli's navy blue hair as he ate me out like I was a glass of water in a desert. I gasped when Eli hit a nerve that I didn't even know I had. Eli lifted his head and he looked up at me with his thick lashes.

"You taste like honey. I could do this all night," he told me.

"Aren't you meant to be making me orgasm?" I teased.

Eli raised an eyebrow and sat on his knees. He placed two fingers inside of me, his other hand resting just above my pelvic bone, pushing down. His fingers moved in and out. I'd never felt anything like it before; the pleasure was more intense than anything I had experienced. I moaned, my eyes rolling back into my head from the knot that was building inside of me.

Eli easily slipped in another finger, then three. I was beginning to feel the tight soreness that came with being stretched.

"I wonder if you could fit my entire fist?" Eli mused.

I moaned at the thought of it. It was something that I had never considered before but my mind wondered and I could see it. Laid out before him, ruined and stretched out.

"I can see you on the edge, Daph. Let's get rid of that headache."

I could feel the pressure building in my stomach, the feeling like I was almost going to wet myself. I had an idea of the kind of edge I was about to dive off. Closing my eyes, I allowed my entire body to relax as much as it could. Eli could sense that I was about to come.

He pushed his fingers deeper.

"Come on, baby. Cum for me."

I pushed up my hips involuntarily. My entire body shook and called out as I drenched him. My body went limp. My breathing was unsteady, irregular, and I felt like I was on another planet.

"One down, one more to go." He leaned over and kissed my cheek.

My eyes fluttered open and I blinked twice. "Another?" I whispered

"Happily. Only if you want to. Or we can snuggle up and fall asleep."

"No." I shook my head. "Show me what you've got."

It was all Eli needed to strip himself of his jeans. He knelt between my legs completely naked and leaned down to kiss me; it was short lived and I tried to keep his lips on mine for as long as possible. Carefully, he repositioned my legs for the perfect view of my wet pussy.

My breathing was uneven, watching him closely for his next move.

Eli placed his hands either side of my head, leaving him in the perfect position to slide slowly into me.

I tipped my head back, a whimper escaping my lips. It had only been a few weeks; the sixth night of freshers week had been interesting but the feeling of Eli inside of me was something else entirely. His cock was lightly stretching me out; I could feel how tight I was still against him. Eli's eye almost rolled back into his head and I giggled slightly.

"Shut up, you. You feel so good." Eli slowly pulled out of me and teased me with the head of his cock pushing lightly at my entrance.

I reached up and wrapped my arms around his neck, pulling him down to kiss me. Our slow and consuming kiss was in rhythm with his deep and slow thrusts. It was sobering for both of us and my headache was a forgotten memory as Eli and I broke the sacred flatmate rule. No one else could know what we had done but I was sure it was going to be written all over my face the next morning.

"Fuck," I mumbled against his lips.

"That's one way to describe it," he whispered. "You're addictive, Daph," he moaned as his thrust began gaining pace. He pulled away from our kiss, taking deep breaths as if he was already holding back.

"Shit, this is what I needed," I closed my eyes.

"From the moment I saw you, I wanted to rip your clothes off and maybe I would have if Nate and Aiden hadn't turned up. Or maybe I should have fucked you senseless anyway."

My eyes flashed open and the thought of Nate and Aiden being in the room with us sent a chill down my back. Them watching us, joining us, and it was hard to get out of my head.

"Faster," I moaned. "I want to cum again. *Please* make me cum."

Eli grabbed both of my legs, settling them on his shoulders to give himself a different position. An angle which had me screaming at the top of my lungs when he buried himself deep inside of me. Eli used one hand to cover my mouth and stop any of our guests storming in to rescue me, though they probably couldn't hear us over the music. Eli's pace got faster, beads of sweat on our skin.

I reached down to my clit, my fingers touching his delicate skin as he pulled, feeling the veins under my finger tips. Then I put two fingers over my clit; I began to rub gently, the knot in my stomach twisting, and I was nearly thrown over the edge again.

Eli took his hand from my mouth and gripped my ankles. He pounded into my wet pussy like it was the last thing he would ever do. The cheap university bed was creaking underneath us and I hoped that I wouldn't be explaining to maintenance later how I'd broken it. Eli's grunts and moans were one and the same as he buried himself into me hard and faster. His teasing was long gone.

My own moans were the background noise to his, both of us lost in a state of ecstasy that our sober brains would regret in the morning.

"Fucking hell, Daph. I never want to stop fucking you. Your pussy is the tightest thing I've felt," he groaned.

I rubbed my fingers harder against my clit.

"I can't hold back much longer," I struggled to speak. "I want us to cum together."

"Yes. Yes." He nodded his head. His hair was stuck to his forehead now; small blue marks were running down the side of his face from the fresh dye.

"Together," he whispered, out of breath. He took my legs off his shoulders and bent down to gift me a searing kiss as we were reaching the edge of our control.

"Shit," I mumbled, rubbing myself at the same speed as Eli was fucking me. My entire pussy was soaked and all I could smell was sex in the air.

"On three," Eli groaned.

"Three," I whimpered.

"Two."

"One."

I let go and my pussy constricted tightly around Eli's thick pulsing cock as he filled me with his cum. He almost collapsed on top of me, gasping for air, before slipping out of me and rolling over to the empty side of the bed.

"Holy shit." Eli squeezed his eyes closed and levelled his breathing before he sat up again.

I didn't expect him to position himself between my legs.

"What the hell are you doing?" I asked.

"I'm not finished with you." He smirked and then buried his face between my thighs.

I gasped as he lightly bit down onto my clit. I was already spent, the level of sensitivity was almost crippling. I'd been lucky if I had climaxed with any guy before, most thinking that when they finished, so did the woman.

Eli had pushed me over the edge twice; three almost felt greedy. My flatmate wasn't bothered by the slightest that his cum was leaking from my pussy as he pushed his tongue inside. He used two fingers and pressed lightly on my clit as he used his mouth. I knew then that it wasn't going to take much more to make me cum again. My already swollen clit was screaming for it to stop, along with the soft whimpers that were escaping my mouth as another episode ended on the TV.

I slumped into the bed sheets, allowing myself to be lost in the euphoric feeling that was being fed to me. Eli lifted his head from my pussy, his lips damp from us both. His two fingers slipped inside of me, curling his fingers as his mouth latched on to my nipple. I gasped at his teeth touching the sensitive skin. He used his tongue, swirling it over my hard nipple, and I pushed my head back into the pillow, moaning.

Eli worshipped each part of my body, teasing me to the edge once more. My mind was floating away from me and all I could think about was how good I was feeling. Aiden 'sending' me to bed was the best thing that was going to happen all year.

"That's it, baby," Eli whispered against my skin. "One more time for me. Please."

I nodded, unable to speak. A broken moan escaped my mouth and I buried my hands into the sheets, twisting the fabric; I couldn't hold back any longer.

Eli didn't stop as I climaxed; he kept going, using his fingers at an insane pace. That had me screaming out. This time, Eli didn't cover my mouth; he was too busy with his own, biting down on my nipple and gifting me another wave of pleasure that had my head spinning. My entire body was shaking as I came down from my high. He kissed my breast and lifted his head to look at me.

"How's the headache?" He smirked again, pulling out his fingers and licking them clean.

I stared at him speechless, giving a small nod; my eyelids were getting heavy as exhaustion hit me.

"Gone," I whispered.

He used his clean hand to cup my cheek and place a gentle kiss on my lips, lingering over the top of me before stealing another.

"I'll clean you up and then you can get some sleep, yeah, baby?"

I nodded as I closed my eyes.

I was asleep before Eli came back.

chapter five

When I woke up the next morning, I was alone, still dressed in Eli's shirt.

Immediately, my mouth was like sandpaper and was begging for water. I snatched the empty cup off my desk and grabbed a glass of water from my en suite. I went to the toilet and it gave me a second to think; I had to talk to Eli and get everything cleared up, make sure that we didn't blow up the peace we had going on.

I flushed the toilet and looked in the mirror. My make up was all over my face, black streaks from the tears that had left my eyes as I came over Eli's tongue. The worst bit of it all is that part of me didn't feel the slightest bit bad about what we had done but it couldn't happen again.

So I took my phone off the bedside table and texted Eli. We couldn't let the others know what we had done; it could ruin the dynamic that we had going and that was the last thing I wanted when cracks were already showing in other flats. Madi was losing her mind over the bitchy girls that she had been placed with.

Daph: Are you awake?

I only waited a few seconds for a reply.

Eli: Yeah I'm awake.

Daph: We should talk about last night...

Eli: Yeah guess we should, come to my room.

Daph: Okay.

I got up and took a new top and pair of leggings from my wardrobe, keeping Eli's shirt in my hands. I walked out into the quiet hallway and knocked on his door. I could hear him getting up and the sound of the latch being unlocked. He pulled open the door wide enough for me to step in.

The layout of his room was familiar, and not just because it was a carbon copy of mine, but because I'd spent countless hours lounging in his room and helping with his essays. I walked down the narrow walkway and into the main space of his room. It was filled with various sound equipment and records, the whole room dedicated to his music degree.

I placed his shirt on the back of his desk chair.

"I brought back your shirt." I turned around, tapping it.

Eli was topless which made it harder to concentrate on what I wanted to say. He sat down on his bed.

"Thanks." He smiled.

I leaned against the wall and looked down at my feet with a bad polish job.

"So last night…It was a bad idea. We have it good, we all get along, and I'd hate for whatever happened to end in tears." I blurted out. My stomach churned for a moment at the thought of this all coming to blows. Protecting myself, I wrapped one arm around myself and lifted my hand to chew on my nails.

"Yeah, I get what you mean. But I don't regret what happened last night; it was good and we're good, you know?"

"I know but what happens if we argue one time and then this all goes to hell? It's just safer if we pretend that this never happened. You're one of my best friends." I looked up and Eli nodded.

"And you're one of mine," he answered. "Don't worry; it won't change anything."

"Okay good. I'm gonna go look at what needs to be cleaned up and cook some breakfast." I pushed off the wall.

Eli leaned over and grabbed his shirt from the chair, putting it back on before standing up. Despite telling him we had to stay as friends, there was something disappointing about him getting dressed; I could no longer admire him.

"Here, I'll come help you." He smiled.

"Okay." Looking into Eli's eyes, I knew I was utterly screwed.

It didn't take us long to tidy up, less than an hour between us. I still found myself trying to avoid him as much as I could as we cleaned. Then, on cue, Nate and Aiden walked in after everything was sparkling and the place smelled like bleach.

"Morning." Nate yawned, taking a seat at one of the stools. "How are you guys feeling?"

"I'm good, a bit fuzzy, that's about it." Eli shrugged, opening the fridge to dig out the bacon.

"Just dehydrated," I answered, pulling out two extra plates from the cupboard. "You guys want a bacon sandwich?"

"You're the best." Aiden smirked, leaning on the island counter. "We're lucky to have you."

"And don't you forget it." I smiled back.

While I helped Eli make breakfast, we kept glancing at each other. Loaded glances that would have told everyone what happened last night if they'd noticed. And that was the last thing I wanted to happen.

It would end in tears.

My tears, to be exact.

chapter six

I WAS TIRED; THE weeks of partying and drinking were taking a toll on me and I couldn't take anymore of it. And that's why I got changed into a fresh pair of pjs while the boys got ready for their night out that Madison was joining them on.

There was a knock on my door and I shouted for them to come in. Aiden strolled into my room with two bottles of aftershave in his hand.

"Help me pick?" He was dressed in a navy t-shirt and his favourite black jeans. His black hair was styled away from his face and his green eyes were still sober and bright.

I stood and took both bottles out of his hand. One was Dior Sauvage and the other a faded Chanel bottle. I raised my brows at him.

"Fancy, are we?" I smirked.

"They were presents." He rolled his eyes. Both of the lids were off and I raised the Dior to my nose, then the Chanel. I handed him back the Chanel and sprayed him with the Dior.

"There's something nice about this one. I've always liked it," I told him.

"You coming out while we have a couple of drinks? I can make you a green tea." He tucked a piece of damp hair behind my ears and I looked up at him. His green eyes twinkled as he dropped his hand.

"Yeah, I'd like that." It was too easy to get lost in any of them. Ever since I'd crossed the line with Eli, it was getting harder and harder to keep myself listening to my brain. The way they treated me felt different, almost like they were feeding me with affection. Maybe they always had been and I was just more paranoid now.

I followed Aiden to the kitchen and pulled myself up onto the island counter. Nate was pouring three whiskey and cokes while Eli played around with his speaker. I watched as Aiden pulled out my favourite cup and put the kettle on for me.

"You sure you don't want to come out with us?" Nate asked.

"I think my liver needs a break," I joked. "But promise me that you guys will keep an eye on Madison? You know what she's like; she runs off and then it takes hours to find her."

"We promise to look after her." Eli touched my arm and took a seat at the island with his drink.

"Okay, you guys better, else you can all do the cleaning for the next month and I mean it."

The kettle popped and Aiden poured the hot water into my mug, along with a spoonful of honey. He passed me it with a teaspoon and the tea bag was still in there.

I thanked him, grateful that he knew exactly how I liked my tea.

"We aren't gonna lose her." Nate backed up Eli's earlier comment.

"We know she's your best friend and we have her back from any creeps, we promise."

Eli's party music played low on his speaker as the boys sat around with their old-man-whiskey. I admired them; there was a part of me that felt something for all of them, they were my best friends. I hadn't had anyone close even back home. Moving here had been my fresh start, as scary as it was. Aiden, Nate and Eli made me happy on a daily basis; I didn't want to have to pick between them.

I took a longer look at Eli. I was starting to miss the way he had touched me and made me feel. The thought of him pulling other girls tonight made my stomach churn. The same with Nate and Aiden. I wanted to be selfish and keep them all to myself. I'd already broken the promise to myself: don't cross the line with the people you lived with. Nevermind the fact that it wasn't only one of them that had caught my eye but three. Something niggled in the back of my mind that it was okay, as long as it didn't change anything, but nothing would stop the pressing anxiety that I'd lose my friends.

The flat door opened and Madison strolled in with her hair curled, lips dipped in red lipstick wearing a white crop top and blue jeans. Her favourite heeled boots were on her feet and I knew she was wearing at least two pairs of socks because they were a little big on her.

"Hello, party boys. Can someone pass me a glass?"

Aiden took a tumbler glass off the draining board and passed it to her. Madison poured her cheap wine and placed the bottle on the side.

"I can't believe you're not coming with us." She pouted, then took a sip of her wine.

"My liver needs a break." I shrugged. "But please promise me that you're gonna stay with the boys tonight."

"You act like I always get lost." She rolled her eyes.

"You *do* always get lost." I laughed.

"Okay, okay, I do. But I won't tonight; I'll be on my best behaviour." She shook me by the shoulders, laughing.

Once the boys and Madison were gone, I got myself into bed with a fresh cup of black tea and biscuits. I turned on my TV and put the latest episode of Eastenders on. It wasn't long though until I fell to sleep.

Only the sound of my phone ringtone woke me and I struggled to peel myself out of the cocoon I had ended up in. I reached over for my phone, my eyes squeezed shut from the brightness.

"Daphne, baby!" Eli slurred down the phone.

"Eli, shut the fuck up," I groaned. Then, I had the sudden fear of Eli telling Nate and Aiden what we had done. I shot up in my bed. "You better not have told anyone."

"Shh. It's a secret." There were more voices in the background. "Can you let us in? We forgot our keys."

"Yeah. Give me a second." I yawned, hanging up on him and stumbling out of bed half asleep. I put on my slippers and picked up a jacket from the mess of clothes on my floor.

How I even found anything in my room was beyond me with two weeks worth of clothes scattered around.

When I opened the front door, there was no one there. I put the door on the latch and wrapped my jacket around me as I walked into the stairwell. The numbers on the lift were not moving and I wondered where the hell Eli was.

There were faint noises coming from the stairwell and I peered over the bannister. Olivia was crawling up the stairs on her hands and knees. Before I could take the piss out of her, I spotted Eli and Nate right behind her.

There were two things that ran through my mind: why were they with Olivia and,

"Where the fuck is Madison?" I folded my arms.

Eli paused on the steps.

Nate moved very slowly, wobbling from his alcohol intake.

Olivia pulled herself up and stood face to face.

"Probably being a bitch like you," she snapped in my face; then, she attempted to push past me but ended up knocking herself into the wall.

I sniggered under my breath as she tried to make her way to her front door.

"Get some new insults already," I called after her, then I turned back to the boys. "Well?"

"So here's the thing…" Eli started, putting his hands up in defence. "It's not like we can go into the toilet with her."

"And then she kinda went poof," Nate finished as he joined me at the top of the stairs.

"For fuck's sake," I sighed. "Come on, I need to call her." I turned and walked back into the flat.

Eli and Nate followed me but I dipped quickly into my room to grab my phone. I pulled up Madison's name in my phone and the call just rang out.

"Fuck," I mumbled and I walked back out to the hallway where the boys were waiting for me like scolded children. "She's not answering. Where's Aiden?" There weren't many words to describe how pissed off I was that they had lost Madison. Alongside that was the dread I was feeling that my best friend was roaming around drunk and alone.

"He went to meet some of his friends from class."

"Can you call him and see if he can find her where he is?" I asked, trying to ring her. No answer.

"Yeah, sure," Eli answered, scrambling to get his phone out.

"We're sorry; we really didn't mean to."

"It's fine. I'm just worried that she's on her own." I raked my fingers through my hair.

"Come on, let's make a cup of tea." Nate nodded towards the kitchen and I followed after him. There wasn't much else I could do which only made me feel uneasy.

I pulled myself up onto the counter and tried calling Madison again. Nothing. I placed my phone down on the side as Nate flicked the kettle on. I watched him as he pulled out three mugs. Sugar. Tea bag. Wait for the kettle. He leaned against where the sink was and pulled out his phone.

"Are you okay?" Eli nudged me, his hand resting on my thigh for a moment too long. The memory of how he felt against me returned to the forefront of my mind and I could have melted into him so easily. But then I remembered who he had returned home with.

"What were you doing with Olivia?" I spoke softly, crossing the line and wanting to claim him for myself, even though I couldn't.

"Jealous?"

Aiden, Nate and Eli had all been furious when they found out what Olivia and her bitches had done in the toilets. The last thing I had expected was to see her with them; it felt like a betrayal.

"Eli." I glared. My mind wandered, imagining her hands all over him, Eli pleasing her like he had me. I was constantly breaking my own rules for someone who could never be mine.

"She was climbing out of her taxi as we got out of ours. We weren't with her. I promise." His thumb stroked the fabric of my pj bottoms with fluffy clouds. I moved his hand away and placed it on the counter before Nate looked up and saw.

"Okay." I nodded. The kettle boiled and Nate poured the hot water into the mugs then grabbed the milk from the fridge. He finished our cups of tea very slowly because of how intoxicated he was; this made me giggle, knowing he was going to be very hungover and I would take pleasure in that. He passed me my mug with two hands and I took it from him.

"Thanks."

I tried to ring Madison for almost an hour as I nursed the tea. Nate had also made the three of us toast. While we were all eating, the front door opened and in strolled a surprisingly sober Aiden with a half eaten kebab. He furrowed his eyebrows at all of us in the kitchen.

"Hey," he spoke.

Eli and Nate greeted him but I only offered a face of stone.

"Everything good?" he asked, stepping into the kitchen.

"You lost Madison," I told him. "You ditched this pair and they lost her which means you lost her too."

"Fuck," he said, placing his kebab on one of the stools.

"Yeah, fuck, and she won't answer her phone."

"How long have you been trying?" he asked.

"About an hour," Nate answered.

Eli rubbed my back and I sighed.

"Let's keep trying," Aiden answered, walking towards me. He brushed my hair back and my heart fluttered.

Gulping, I tried to keep my brain focused on getting hold of Madison. I picked up my phone again to try calling her. The dial tone against my ear and on the eighth ring she finally picked up; I jumped off the counter.

"Madi, where are you?!" I pushed past Aiden and stood where I had space to freak out by the sofas.

"I'm on campus." She whispered it so quietly that I could barely hear her.

"What? Why?"

"Well he was cute and he made me toast."

"Okay, you need to get in a taxi; you're scaring me. Why on earth are you whispering?" I asked, glancing at Nate and Eli who were listening in.

"He's in the bathroom, cleaning up. We made a mess."

I burst out laughing.

"Jesus, Madi. Okay, can you get home?"

"Does she need us to come get her?" Aiden asked.

"The boys can come get you."

"I'm okay," she said softly. "I will get a taxi."

"Now?" I asked.

"Yeah, yeah; I love you so much my pretty friend, mwah, mwah, mwah."

"Please text me."

"I will, gotta go." Madison hung up and I took a deep breath, happy that she was safe.

For the next twenty minutes, I made sure the boys knew that just because she was okay, it didn't mean they weren't complete idiots and I was still pissed at them.

I relaxed finally when Madison texted me when she was pulling into the car park. Aiden and Eli offered to walk down and meet her, feeling guilty they had lost her. I let out a sigh of relief when they walked in with Madison following close behind.

"She wanted to stay with you," Aiden told me.

Madison fell into me and wrapped her arms around my body.

"I love you for caring so much about me," she mumbled.

"Of course I do, you're my best friend," I told her. "Come on, let's go chill." I pulled away from her and looked at my three flatmates.

"Night, Daph." Nate smiled back.

"Goodnight." Eli nodded at me.

"Sweet dreams, girls," Aiden called.

"Night, guys," I spoke bluntly. The microwave was still propping the door open so I kicked it out of the way so the door would shut dramatically behind me.

I helped Madison into a spare pair of my pjs and we both got into my bed. We lay side by side, looking at one another.

"I'm such an idiot; I don't even know who that guy was," she groaned.

"You're not an idiot, go you for getting what you needed," I joked. But I chewed on my lip; I had to tell someone about what happened with Eli and I before I exploded. "You know Olivia wasn't really wrong…I slept with Eli."

Madison shot up in bed.

"You what? When?" It was almost like she had completely sobered herself up.

I sat up too.

"The other week at the flat party, we were both drunk. I had a headache and well... he offered to help get rid of it."

"That smooth bastard," she laughed. "Was he good? I bet he's good. He has to be. Tell me everything." Madison lay back down.

And before I got to tell her even half of what happened, she was dead asleep in an alcohol-induced coma.

chapter seven

Was I the luckiest girl alive? I didn't hear one complaint from any of the boys as we walked around the shopping centre. Nate had even offered to hold my bags. They all quietly stood behind me as I examined the silver rings that were being displayed in the window.

The urge to splash some of my student loans had become too much and I was now using my first essay submission as an excuse for a celebration. I'd probably regret it later on but, in the moment, I was happy to shop til I dropped.

"Daph, we're gonna be late for the bottomless brunch, come on." Eli tugged on my arm.

"Okay, okay." I lifted my hands up holding my shopping bags. Aiden reached up and took them from me.

"Here, I'll take those," he said.

"Thanks, Aid." I leaned up and kissed his cheek, locking eyes with him for one second longer than I should have.

When I first suggested bottomless brunch, the boys were completely against it because it sounded 'girly'. That is, until they realised that they could compete with one another on who could drink the most.

We were put into a booth at Turtle Bay. I sat on one side closest to the wall, Eli sat opposite me, his leg touching mine. Nate sat next to Eli and Aiden took the place next to me. We'd all ordered rum punch; I'd chosen to sip mine and enjoy it while the boys tried to get it down as fast as they could.

Nate was multitasking, swiping through his Tinder at the same time. I rolled my eyes at him and snatched his phone.

"Oi," he called me out and I took a look at the girl on the screen.

The pretty blonde was from our uni, in fact, *our* block of flats. I swiped right on her and the match came up instantly. There was a pang in my chest as Nate reached over the table for his phone and took it back.

"You shouldn't be so picky," I chuckled at him, laughing off the pain in my chest as I willingly set him up with someone that wasn't me.

"I'm not being picky." He stuck his tongue out like a child.

"Now, now, children, let's not start," Aiden butted in.

Before I could open my mouth again, one of the staff members brought over two of our meals.

" Chicken roti wraps, no avocado and fries?" she asked.

I lifted my hand. "That's mine, thank you."

She leaned over the table; the vest top she was wearing was showing off her chest and I couldn't help but notice her eyes were directly on Aiden as she placed down my plate.

I raised my eyebrow at her, a wave of unexpected jealousy hitting me.

Our eyes met and she quickly cleared her throat and stood back up, announcing the other meal which was Nate's chicken wrap. She scuttled off back to the kitchen. Aiden's hand brushed my shoulder, stroked it even. I looked at him and he smirked at me; he'd noticed my guard routine. My cheeks blushed and I turned to the food in front of me, picking up a chip and dipping it in the pot of mayo. I kept my head down, my cheeks burning and no doubt a rosey red.

It was getting more and more frequent: pure jealousy. First it was when I heard Olivia and her bitch crew in the toilets, then when I saw Olivia with Nate and Eli in the stairwell and lastly when I had come back from class before we went out. Beth had been there, flirting with Aiden because she couldn't open a jar.

"So, it's Friday night; what are we going to be doing?" Eli asked.

"How about pres with just us four and then we head into town tonight?" Aiden suggested. The waitress then came back with the other two plates.

Eli had the jerk beef burger and Aiden had gone for the hot chicken burger. The waitress refused to make eye contact with me or the boys this time around. The blush spread across my cheeks as I thought about how protective I had been again for no reason.

"I don't think my bank account can take another night out," Nate admitted.

"It's a pound a drink at Pryzm tonight; the most you'll spend is ten quid." Eli nudged him. "You know you don't want to stay in all night."

"Come on, I'll buy you some shots." I reached out to touch his hand. We made eye contact and I smiled at Nate.

"Okay, fine."

"Yeah bro, you really needed a lot of persuading," Aidan smirked.

"You can't say no to free shots." He shrugged, taking a bite of a chunky chip from his plate. "Plus, have you seen that face?" He gestured to me and I grinned at all three boys, causing them to laugh at me.

I knew I was beyond lucky that I had ended up placed with people I loved to hang out with, unlike the rest of the building who were constantly falling out and screaming at one another. *They* were nothing like me and my boys, as long as I never let what happened between me and Eli happen again. And, somehow, I needed to get my jealousy under control.

chapter eight

IF THERE WAS ONE thing that I hated, it was my Wednesday timetable: 9 to half 5 was packed with classes. I knew that it was nothing compared to shifts that people put in at work but when the rest of my days consisted of only a couple of hours, I questioned why they filled just one entire day of bullshit.

I yawned as I twisted the key into the front door; it had taken me almost an hour to walk back and I was so ready for bed. At least when I was asleep I didn't think of my stupid mistake with Eli. I pushed open the door. The hallway light was on and the kitchen door was shut. Instead of heading straight for my room like I should have, I walked into the kitchen and nearly wanted to throw up at the sight in front of me.

Beth was sitting on my kitchen counter, her legs wrapped around Nate. Their mouths locked together. She'd finally got her red claws into one of them. My blood boiled at the sight of them entwined; my jealousy would have made more sense if it were Eli being pounced on but jealousy spread to each one of my flatmates when it came to the bitches next door. Her hands were wrapped into the hair of the back of his neck, his hands planted either side of her, only his thumbs touched her thighs.

Beth's eyes opened and they locked with mine. I narrowed my own and stepped out, slamming the door shut.

I spun around to head back to my room, instead coming face to face with Eli. He gripped my arms.

"Are you okay?"

"Yeah. Lost my appetite but that happens when your friend is eating a bitch's face off." I pulled out of his touch and walked towards my door. I'd left it unlocked which meant Eli didn't have time to pull me back.

When I was safe inside of my room, I threw my bag down on the floor and kicked off my shoes. I raked my hair back and screamed behind clenched teeth. One day, that bitch is throwing herself over Aiden cause she couldn't open a jar, then the next she was eating Nate's face off. I felt sick to my stomach.

I had to clear my head. I pulled my jumper over my head, taking off my jeans then vest and finally grabbing my towel.

After stripping off my underwear, I flipped on the shower in my en suite and let the hot water uncurl every inch of my tense body. But I couldn't stop thinking about them, in the kitchen, metres away from me. My brain wouldn't stop.

Trying to distract myself again, I grabbed my loafer and shower gel, squirting a small amount. I lathered up the soap under the water stream and ran it down my arms. I massaged the soap into my skin, zoned out into a spot on the small cubicle. They'd probably taken it to Nate's room by now. He would have undressed her, holding her close, making her feel like she was the only woman in the world. I knew that because Nate was a player. Yet I still found myself burning with jealousy and the hot water burning my skin.

It should have been me.

My heart was wrestling with my brain. I'd already had Eli and, despite us not making the same mistake again, I'd claimed him. He was mine. And my greed was begging for Nate too.

I brushed over my chest, grazing my nipples that were hardening from the thought of having Nate. I removed Beth from my mind and just thought about him. The things he could do to me.

The way he'd kiss me so forcefully… I'd melt.

I moved the loafer lower down, across my stomach.

I imagined him throwing me on the bed.

I shut my eyes and leaned against the cold shower tiles. I moved closer and closer to where the ache between my legs was firing up and I knew there was no going back. The loafer dropped to the floor, my fingers dancing over my bare pussy as my mind was filled with everything that I wanted Nate to do to me. Pinned down to the mattress, letting him have his way with me. Eli had worshipped *me* but I wanted to worship *Nate*.

I slipped my fingers down, touching my wet clit, gently rubbing circles around it, chewing my lip and enjoying the flickers of pleasure in the pit of my stomach. I wanted to feel him inside of me, hard for me, just for me.

Eli had been impressive so I knew that Nate would be just as big.

I slipped two fingers inside of myself, burying them as deep as I wanted Nate to be inside of me and propping my leg against the wall for an easier angle.

I knew exactly where to curl my fingers to make my legs shiver to the point where I thought I was going to slip. I imagined Nate in the shower with me, holding me up in the tight space, using every inch of space we had left to thrust up inside of me. He would pound into me so hard that all we would be able to hear over the shower was the sound of our bodies together.

"Fuck," I mumbled under my breath. The knot in my stomach twisted with every curl. The need was almost consuming; I was on the edge and it only took the thought of remembering what it felt like to have Eli between my legs to throw me over.

There was no stopping my screaming as I slumped to the floor with my fingers still buried inside myself. My chest was almost thumping out of my chest and I couldn't hear anything but the blood pumping around my body. Shakily, I reached up and turned off the shower, even though I still had soap on my body. There was no way I could stand and that was only from *thinking* about Nate. I dreaded to know what it would do to me if Nate *really* fucked me.

chapter nine

THAT NIGHT I COULDN'T sleep. Thinking about Nate in the shower had made me sick once I'd come down from the high. I threw off my duvet, grabbed my phone and stepped over my various dirty clothes lying on the ground.

I had to clear my head and the only thing that would do that is chocolate. I tiptoed down to the kitchen, only opening the door a small amount to slip in. I reached over in the dark to turn the light on.

"Okay, chocolate," I told myself and began to rummage around the cupboards for the ingredients to make brownies. Sugar. Flour. Cocoa powder. I got the butter from the fridge and because it was his fault, I took one of Nate's many eggs.

As I baked, I played an episode of 'Buffy the Vampire Slayer' for my 'Monsters, Cyborgs, and Imaginary Worlds' class. There was no need for me to look at the instructions; I'd baked them so many times now.

I looked over my shoulder when I heard the door open. Aiden walked in. His light brown hair was messy and all he was wearing was his navy blue joggers. I gave him a tired smile and carried on stirring.

"Here, let me help," he offered.

I nodded and stepped aside. Aiden picked up the spoon and carried on stirring but then glanced at my phone.

"Where are you at now?" he asked.

"Angel just got his soul taken away. And now he's an ass." I pulled myself up on the counter.

"My mom was always a big Angel fan."

"All moms are Angel fans."

"So, what's got you making brownies at one in the morning?"

"Couldn't sleep." It wasn't necessarily a lie. Aiden turned around and took the pre-heated metal tin out of the oven with the glove before starting to pour the batter.

"Okay but why?" he asked me.

"I came in from class earlier and Nate was making out with Beth on the-" Realising that I was sitting in the spot where Beth had been earlier, a shiver ran down my spine. "-side."

"Hmm, I thought she was after Eli."

I glared at him.

"She's after anything that breathes, just like the rest of them," I scoffed.

Aiden handed me the spoon to lick; like he knew that chocolate would stop me from turning into a murderer. I poked my tongue out to taste a little of the chocolate, moaning to myself which landed Aiden's eyes right on me. I blushed.

"After what Olivia and her bitches did too, which includes Beth." I frowned.

"He wouldn't have done it to upset you," he told me, putting my brownies in the oven.

"I'm not upset," I lied. Partially, because it had turned me on enough that I came thinking about him.

Aiden threw the oven gloves on the side and leaned against the sink with his arm crossed, defining the outline of his muscular arms.

"No, of course you're not. That's why you're baking brownies and your face is still sour."

I leaned over and turned my phone off.

"You know, if you're going to just insult me, you can go join Nate in his love nest and leave me alone." I attempted to walk away and, as I reached for the door handle, Aiden grabbed me by the wrist and pulled me back again.

We were almost nose-to-nose, except Aiden was taller than me.

"I'm not insulting you, I just know the truth. You're easy to read. I know it must have upset you because of what Olivia and the others did."

"Then why did he do it?" I locked eyes with his pretty boyish green ones and took a deep breath.

"Because he's an idiot but don't hold it against him. You tend to make people do crazy things," he whispered and I swore his head dipped towards mine, our noses side by side, our lips almost grazing against one another. His hot breath intertwined with mine.

Then his hand moved from my wrist, gliding further up my arm, towards my neck until his thumb was brushing my cheek. I took a step back; a deer caught in headlights would have described me at that moment. And I ran. Down the hallway and into the comfort of my four walls.

When I went to check on my brownies fifteen minutes later, Aiden was gone.

chapter ten

Monday nights were the biggest in town: almost every club offered deals which ended up with students rolling into class the next day hungover. Not that any student really cared about that; even I wondered how I was still getting good grades with the amount of times I had turned up with my sunglasses on. Letting loose and dancing all night gave me the opportunity to have fun and forget the pressures of the stack of reading I had or the looming essay that was due in a week.

I swayed my hips to the beat of the music, moving with Madison who we had bumped into. My heels were uncomfortably sticking to the floor because of the spilled drinks and my hair was beginning to sweat on the back of my neck; I knew my makeup would be next. I turned around to Madison and called down her ear.

"I'm going to find the boys, I'm sweating!" I shouted.

Madison nodded and kissed my cheek.

"Stay here; don't be getting lost," I warned her playfully.

She smiled and shrugged at me. I rolled my eyes and shook my head.

"I promise I'll stay here!" she shouted back.

I raised my brow at her.

"I promise! I'll go find the girls." Meaning others from our class, who I knew were a lot more sober than Madison was.

"Okay, I'll be back soon!"

I pulled my heels up from the sticky dance floor and stepped back onto the carpet, trying to push myself through the crowd of people as I made my way towards the exit for the smoking area. Eli had needed a breather and Nate had wanted to vape; all three of them ended up leaving me with Madison. And my dependence on them didn't like that.

I made the final push through the crowd. The freshness hit me and I was breathing air rather than BO, although the air outside was still polluted with smoke. I stepped onto my tiptoes, searching the crowd of people socialising while they smoked and vaped. I looked to my left and smiled at the security guard; he was watching me carefully.

The boys were standing in a far corner talking with a few other people. I walked as slowly and calmly as possible in case I tripped up and was thrown out for being too drunk. Eli was the first to spot me and smiled; our eyes met and I was reminded of the way my body shivered when he had made me come.

I pulled my eyes away and they landed on the people they were with which included Olivia and Elisha. There were a couple of others from our block too; I assumed that's why they were even there. My heart thumped; they looked stunning. I looked down at my long sleeved black dress and felt boring as hell.

I didn't like the way Elisha was flirting with Eli. My teeth grinned together, my mind screaming that I should mark my territory. I had to remind myself that Eli wasn't mine and I couldn't have him, at least without it going completely wrong in a few weeks' time.

I stood next to Nate who kissed the top of my head. Another shiver ran down my spine. He didn't know that I had seen him with Beth who thankfully wasn't anywhere to be seen. I'd tried to keep my distance since then. I glanced at

Aiden; I'd pretty much avoided him too but, when needed, I was good at putting on an act. Although, it wasn't an act that all three boys were my knights in shining armour.

"Hey, Daph."

"Hey," I said, wrapping my arms around my body to protect myself from the cold.

Nate took one glance at me, rolling his eyes. He pulled me in front of him and opened up his jacket, wrapping me inside of it. Instinctively, I relaxed into his chest as I watched Elisha play with Eli's hair. My jaw clenched and I started to grind my teeth as Nate lowered his mouth to my ear.

"Careful, sweetheart, before you burn a hole into the back of her head."

I blinked twice and turned my eyes to another group of people.

"I don't know what you're going on about." I shrugged, resting my head against his collarbone.

"Please; you and Eli have been itchy around each other for weeks. I think something went on or you *want* something to go on," he spoke low in my ear. He didn't know half of it and that *he* was another half.

Aiden put out his cigarette on the ground with his eyes directly on Nate and I. I smiled at him, trying to not remember how we'd almost kissed last week.

I involuntarily yawned and covered my mouth.

"Well, that's Daph out for the count," Nate chuckled.

I jabbed my elbow into him.

"It's nearly three anyway." Aiden shrugged. "One of us can take you home."

"I'll do it," Eli offered and I rolled my eyes despite my internal protest. Elisha was still standing beside him and I wanted nothing more to get her claws out of him.

"I can get myself into a taxi," I told the three of them, pulling myself from the warmth of Nate's jacket.

"You're wasted, like we'd let you go home alone." Aiden shook his head.

"I'm not a child and I've done it before."

"What do you mean you've done it before?" He folded his arms.

"You're not on every night out with me; how do you think I get home? I'll be fine." I stalked off in my heels before any of them could say anything. My blood was boiling from either jealousy or alcohol consumption. But as I stepped into the building again, someone grabbed my arm.

I whipped around ready to punch whoever it was in the face. Nate was the one who had grabbed me; the security guard that was keeping an eye on the smoking area stood to attention and I gave him a friendly smile to let him know that he didn't need to do anything.

"Come on, green-eyed monster; I'm done for the night anyway."

I went to open my mouth but decided against it, knowing it would make things a whole lot worse.

Nate walked behind me but in close proximity, his hands placed firmly on my waist as we made our way through the crowd between the bar and the dance floor. The music was still thumping and people were crammed together; I spotted Madison as she made her way to the bar for another round. I reached out and grabbed her arm. She spun around ready to kick off at whoever grabbed her, until she realised it was me.

"I'm heading home!" I shouted down her ear. "Stay with the rest of the girls okay? Call me if you need me!"

"Okay, text me when you're home!" she shouted back.

Nate tugged me away from Madison as I blew her a kiss.

The best part about the city was how small it was, meaning we could walk home without spending money on taxis.

I enjoyed the lights and the old buildings with small details that gave them character.

For a while, there was a heavy silence between us as I chewed on my lip.

"I'm not a green-eyed monster, you know?" I blurted out, whipping my head around to face him as we reached the main gate of our housing.

Nate blinked and his drunk mind took a moment to process what I'd said and *why*.

"Oh yeah? None of us are blind, Daph," he chuckled and shook his head as we walked towards our building.

"Clearly, you are," I mumbled. *Clearly*, I was lying to myself. We approached the front door of our building and I leaned against the glass window as Nate fumbled around trying to find his keys and fob.

Opposite us was the smoking area where a group of students were laughing and drinking from cans, music blaring from a speaker that sounded like nails on a chalkboard. One spotted me and with a lopsided grin, he whistled at me. Nate looked over his shoulder and glared, reaching over to cover my cleavage as he used the fob to let us into the building. He ushered me into the lobby.

"Now who's the green-eyed monster?" I smirked, pressing the lift button; the doors opened instantly. I stepped in and Nate joined me.

It wasn't until the doors shut that my breath was taken from me. I was pushed against the cold, metal wall of the lift... Nate pinning me by the throat, his thigh between my legs and riding up my dress. I took a deep breath as he lightly squeezed my neck and leaned closer.

"At least I'll admit it." His lips brushed against the curve of my ear, then he pulled away, loosening his . With his spare hand, he pressed the button to our floor.

"Admit what? You're too busy fucking the whores next door to even look at me."

"Is that what you think?" He pressed his forehead against mine. "Have you ever thought for one second that the reason I have to go somewhere else is because I can't have you?"

I was stunned, a deer caught in headlights.

"What?" I mumbled.

Nate pressed his lips against mine. His kiss was consuming and hungry. While Eli had been almost sweet, Nate had my knees trembling. He squeezed my neck lightly and a small whimper escaped my lips. My flatmate bit my lower lip, releasing another.

The lift stopped and Nate released my neck. I placed my hand on my chest, taking a moment to catch my breath.

We stepped out and once again Nate grabbed me, cupping my face with his hands as he directed me backwards towards our front door. His lips never left mine as he fumbled with his keys with one hand, my head pressed against the door. I wrapped my arms around his neck as we stumbled into the flat.

Once we were inside, Nate used his hands to tug my dress up to my hips and grabbed two handfuls of my lace-decorated ass.

"Jump," he breathed heavily against my lips before capturing me in another consuming kiss. I did as he requested and jumped, wrapping my legs around his middle. Carrying me into the bedroom, Nate threw me down on his bed, causing me to gasp. He took no time to take off my heels and then slid my underwear down my legs. I propped myself up on my elbows and gulped, looking at him as he looked at me like a three-course meal. "Dress off and anything else. I want it all off," he ordered. I sat up and quickly took off my dress and then my black lacy bra.

I was completely bare in front of him and Nate leaned against his wall, palming his jeans that were straining against the bulge. I offered a small smile to calm my nerves. Nate pulled off his shirt and disappeared from my eyesight for a moment. I heard the lock click and there was no turning back; there was no denying that I was ending up completely spent because of my jealous housemate.

Nate appeared again, shirtless, and the button of his jeans undone.

"Get on your knees, Daph."

I nodded frantically. The cold air had not only brought up goosebumps on my arms but my nipples were rock solid. I lowered myself onto the rough cheap carpet and looked up at him. Nate shoved his jeans down his thighs and I helped guide them to his ankles. He was wearing grey boxers which showed the small patch of pre-cum that had soaked through. I examined the hard-line trapped by the thin fabric, tilting my head ever so slightly. Then, I shakily hooked my fingers into his boxers, tugging them down. His hard and thick cock flicked up to his stomach. I had no doubts though that he would be able to ruin me just as much as Eli had that night, if not more.

I leaned forward, taking the tip of his cock into my mouth and gently sucking on it, my eyes locked with his as I took him further into my mouth. Nate threw his head back as my tongue ran under his swollen head.

"Fucking hell, sweetheart." He took a fistful of my hair, tight enough that it stung a little which only powered me further to take him down to the base.

My gag reflex didn't fail me but my jaw ached. There was no stopping my mouth from watering. Nate used my hair to pull me back and slam my mouth back down on his dick again and again. Rough and hard, the jealousy from the guys downstairs took over him; it meant he was desperate to prove a point which included whatever he had spotted going on between Eli and I.

"That's my girl, keep doing that."

I carried on, using my tongue on the sensitive under head and balancing myself by holding onto his thighs.

He was beginning to tremble, tightening in my mouth, ready to fill it with every last drop. His fingers gripped my hair tighter as he forced himself to pull my lips off his cock.

"Not yet," he panted. "I need you. Fuck, sweetheart, I need you." He let go of my hair and ran his thumb over my swollen bottom lip.

I stood and Nate pulled me in by the waist for another demanding kiss, pressing my body against his hard cock which made the wetness between my legs spread to my thighs. I moaned against his lips.

"Then have me," I whispered. Nate shook off his jeans and boxers without breaking contact, then threw me down on his bed. Nate pulled down the bed, spreading my knees apart so that he could position himself between them.

In one swift motion, Nate was buried inside of me and my whimper bounced off the walls as he took a sigh of relief. He leant down and kissed me, softer than before as he began to thrust slow and deep inside of me. Small and quiet gasps escaped me as he took my breath away. The feeling of being stretched open by Nate had me wet and my skin on fire.

Nate pulled away, tucking his head into my neck as his thrusts got harder and faster, taking my breath away again and again. His lips attached to the sensitive skin on my neck and lightly nipped, marking me. I panicked and pushed him away. Nate lifted his head.

"No marks. I don't want anyone to know. Please. It could mess up the whole flat."

"Okay, guess I'll just do it where no one can see then." Nate lowered himself slightly, still pumping into me as he latched onto my tit and bit harder than he had on my neck. I moaned and lifted my hand to tug on his hair. The pressure in my stomach was starting to build and I was internally already begging for the release... to clench around him and make Nate fill me up the same way Eli had.

I was jealous and greedy and protective.

I wanted Eli and I wanted Nate. I even wanted Aiden because they were *my* men. I was greedy because I didn't want to pick.

Nate came up for air and I dipped my eyes to see the already purpling bite on my skin. He returned to my lips, his thrusts changing, slamming into my wet pussy hard and slowly retreating over and over again. Light spots appeared in my vision and my mind was turning to complete mush as my orgasm built up in my core. My lips were parted as moans escaped my mouth, my tits bounced in the rhythm of Nate's thrusts. I reached up, gripping onto his biceps, my nails digging into his skin. Nate bit his lip and moaned.

"Fucking hell, sweetheart, do you know tight you are, how fuckable your pussy is?" He leant down to kiss me again. "I'm not going to be able to hold back much longer."

"I'm close too, it's okay," I whispered, capturing his lips for a quick kiss.

Nate's thrusts changed to animalistic; they were hard, fast and I could hear the wetness of my pussy in the air as he fucked me into his mattress.

The pressure in my stomach, in my pussy, was too much to handle; I removed my hands from his arms and gripped the sheets, tight enough that my knuckles turned white.

"That's my girl," he panted. A thin layer of sweat had formed on his skin. "Come for me, sweetheart. Please let me feel you cum."

The pet name and the sweet manners set me over the edge and my hips buckled up against me as a flood of pleasure escaped me. I moaned loud enough that the others would have heard us if they were here.

It was all Nate needed for his balls to tighten and fill me full of his warm cum, just like Eli had. His head dropped down when he had finished emptying himself inside of me, taking unsteady breaths as he came down from the high.

Slowly, he pulled out of me and sat back on his knees. His hand dipped between my thighs, using his finger to collect his cum and lifted his finger to my lips. Instinctively, I parted my mouth and locked eyes with him as he pushed his finger into my mouth. I closed my lips around him and sucked the salty substance from his finger. A small smile danced on his lips, then he pulled his finger from my mouth with a pop.

There was a small moment of silence between us and then we burst into a fit of giggles for twenty seconds straight.

"Can I use your bathroom to clean up? Then I'll go back to my room." I quickly stood up, clenching to stop anything from leaking onto his sheets.

"Sure but you don't have to go back to your room, you know?" He shrugged, bending over to pick up his boxers from the floor.

I smiled at the thought of spending the night. But I knew I couldn't.

I dashed into the bathroom and closed the door. After I cleaned myself up and went to the toilet, I walked back into Nate's bedroom. He was ready to pass me one of his t-shirts and I thanked him.

"So, are you gonna stay?" he asked.

"I-I don't know. Eli or Aiden could come back and start asking questions." I pulled on his shirt; it swamped me, dropping to my mid thigh.

"I have a lock and you know they won't be up til late in the afternoon." Nate pulled me by my hips and looked down at me.

I chewed on my lip, taking a moment to consider it because he wasn't wrong; neither of them would see the morning. I nodded and a smile appeared on Nate's face.

"Hey, this doesn't mean anything, it can't." I wanted it to, but I wanted Eli, which is exactly why I couldn't. This was the problem I didn't want to face: having to choose between any of them because all three of them treated me like I was the most precious thing in the world. It would only end in tears.

"I know." He kissed the top of my head.

"Okay, as long as we're on the same page."

Which was a complete lie because my heart was on a different one to my brain.

chapter eleven

I WOKE UP WRAPPED in Nate's arms in the cool pitch black room. His back was against the wall and mine was tightly held against him. It took me a few moments to peel myself away without disturbing him. I felt around for my dress in the dark and my phone. I still had some battery left and was able to tell the time; it was eight which meant I could easily sneak out of Nate's room without having to answer why I was dressed in his shirt and sneaking out of his room. Especially to Eli because I didn't know how I would even begin to explain without hurting his feelings or my own.

I tiptoed over to the door and carefully pulled down the latch to let myself out. The hallway was just as dark as Nate's room, giving me another layer of protection to get back to my own. I walked down the hall, dodging the spots that

I knew would creak. My hand was on my unlocked door when the hallway light flicked on. I held my breath and turned, my hand still on the door. Standing right outside the kitchen door was Aiden; he was shirtless, holding a glass of water.

"Came to check you were okay when we got back last night," he said. "But you weren't there."

I tried to speak but I stumbled on my words.

"I must have been in the bathroom." I'd been caught red-handed. There was no way of explaining why I was in Nate's t-shirt and sneaking into my room.

"Your own or Nate's?" He took a sip of water.

Jealousy.

That's all that radiated off him.

His jaw was locked, clutching his glass a little too tightly as he looked at me in Nate's shirt. Nothing I hadn't done before; I'd even worn *his* at some point.

Guilt flooded me like nothing before as I remembered how we had almost kissed.

I didn't know how to reply so instead I walked into my room, shut the door and locked it. I pressed my body against my door and slid down the wood. I closed my eyes and took a deep breath.

If Aiden were to say anything, everything would blow up in my face. Flatmate fall-outs had already started happening, even Madison was having a tough time of it. I knew I was lucky and I'd just messed everything up with two really stupid drunk mistakes… only they didn't feel like mistakes at all.

I managed to get some more sleep after I'd pulled myself from the floor. I woke up sweating, though; one of the boys must have turned on the heating. I kicked my covers off and allowed my skin to cool before checking my phone. The group chat was dead and not even Nate had messaged me. It was four in the afternoon; they would have all been up by now which only meant that everything had fallen apart while I was asleep and now I had to deal with the fallout.

Which I avoided… taking a shower and letting the hot water turn my skin red, ridding myself of the sweat from alcohol and sex. I dug my nails into my scalp as I washed my hair and moaned at the relaxing sensation. My moans caused flashbacks of how Nate had me feel and then Eli. My head was spinning again and I leaned back against the shower wall, closing my eyes to ignore the bright bathroom lighting. I reached out to turn off the shower and it didn't take long for the cool air to hit me.

I got out of the shower, brushed through my hair and put on a hoodie and pair of leggings. My stomach rumbled and I huffed, going over to the snack draw in my room. Which was empty. I slammed it shut.

"For fuck's sake." I looked at my door and felt sick. I was hungry. I could either quickly go into the kitchen and hope that I wouldn't see anyone or head straight for the front door and walk to the shop. Neither were appealing.

I put my door on the latch and scurried down the hallway; I didn't hear voices on the other side of the kitchen door. But as I stood in the doorway frozen, Nate and Eli were looking right at me. My blood ran cold and goosebumps ran up my skin. Whatever they were talking about, they had stopped as soon as I had opened the door and that was all I needed to know that they were talking about me.

"Just grabbing some snacks, heads still banging," I lied, dipping down to my cupboard. I pulled out a couple bars of chocolate and a tube of Pringles. I shot the boys a fake smile and left the room, holding my breath until I was back behind the safety of my door.

I'd fucked everything up.

chapter twelve

IT WAS THE FIRST flat party that I didn't bother going to, even though it was in *my* flat. Over the past few days, there had been some awkward conversations; everyone was feeling the tension or at least I was. I'd overheard Nate saying that I was probably on my period; that just showed me how little he knew about Depo injection. Aiden, on the other hand, I had avoided completely. From his comment in the hall, I knew he was jealous and there was nothing I could do about it because once I'd done it with all of them, I just knew they would make me choose.

I couldn't.

I attempted to bury my head in my essay that was due next week but my procrastination was already hitting me and I knew I'd end up doing it the night before. I'd been doodling on a piece of paper for the past ten minutes, listening to Eli's playlist echoing down the hallway. My lights were dim which was only making me tired.

While I was considering calling it a night, there was a knock on my door. I was running on autopilot and got up to answer it, thinking that it was probably going to be Madison trying to drag me out of my room again like she had only half an hour ago. I'd told her everything when she was sober this time and her face when I told her I'd slept with Nate, Eli and almost kissed Aiden had been priceless.

"Mad-" I said, opening my door. Only it wasn't Madison standing in a pair of black skinny jeans and navy blue t-shirt. It was Aiden. His hair was styled back off his face, showing off his green eyes.

"We need to talk," he spoke and pushed his way in gently; I let him. The door shut as I turned to see him looking over my desk.

"What about?" I swallowed. This was it: nuclear war.

"Nate and Eli, they know you're avoiding them. They've talked and they know you've fucked them both. Not that it was some big secret. Your green eyes are worse than mine and mine are, well, actually green."

I sat on the edge of my bed and looked down at my fuzzy socks.

"I don't know what you want me to say," I whispered, squeezing my eyes shut. There was a moment of silence before there was a tug on my hair, pulled back so I was looking up at Aiden.

"I want you to say it's my turn," he spoke low, looking down at me.

My lips parted in shock and I didn't have much time to process what Aiden had just said before his lips were softly pressed against mine. That was the only moment of softness I was going to get. Five seconds later, Aiden bit down on my lip and tugged my hair, ordering me to stand.

With our lips still connected, I stood and Aiden pushed me against the wall, his hand released from my hair and wrapped around my neck instead.

"Well, are you going to say it?" he whispered, his forehead pressed against mine.

"I've already fucked up twice. I don't want to lose any of you," I replied.

"Not gonna happen. That I can promise you. You just need to open your eyes a little more."

"There's no version of this that someone comes out unscathed." I put my hands on his chest, trying to make some sort of distance between the two of us.

"Stop thinking, stop talking, Daph." He pushed our lips together again, pulling me closer by my neck. His kiss devoured me and any left of brain power I had left. There was something about kissing these boys that made me lose all common sense.

His hand released my neck and darted towards my leggings. He pressed against the fabric, feeling for my clit. I hadn't bothered to wear underwear while I was trying to study and I'd only ended up making it easier for Aiden. His two fingers rubbed slow circles and there was a familiar fluttering in my stomach. I kissed back, properly, giving it my all. My hands reached up to cup his face and I could feel the slight smirk on Aiden's lips as he used his other hand to reach up for my hair again and pull me away from the wall.

The hand rubbing me was getting impatient with the barrier of fabric and dipped into my legs to feel the warm heat that was beginning to radiate from me. One finger dragged between my folds to examine the dampness that he'd created.

Aiden pulled away from my lips which only had me chase them for more. His eyes glanced at my open laptop and textbook as he pulled his fingers from my leggings and put his fingers into his mouth to taste me. My lips parted as I watched him. He turned back and tilted his head. There had always been something underneath Aiden's leadership qualities. He'd taken on the role in the flat dynamic so well and I was about to see the rest of it.

"What were you working on?" he asked.

"Just... just my essay on Shakespeare, the metaphor of the witches in Macbeth," I stumbled out.

"Well, I wouldn't want you not to get your essay in on time; let's make sure you finish it."

My brows furrowed. One minute he was kissing my face off and the next he just wanted me to carry on with my work. It made no sense... until Aiden used my hair to direct me back to my desk and bend me over the back of my chair . I jolted and held onto the desk to balance myself, my position giving him clear access to whatever he wanted of me. Aiden tugged down my leggings and I swallowed.

Using two fingers, he dragged them over my wet fold and teased my clit, then down to my hole where he would dip his fingers in so slightly. I whimpered when I felt his fingers tease the entrance of me and then back up to my clit.

"Go on," he told me, releasing my hair and placing the hand on my back, pushing the chair in a little more, enough for me to easily touch the keyboard. He used his foot to knock my legs further apart. "Keep writing, Daph." This time when he reached my entrance, he pushed his fingers in fully and curled them to hit the spot that had a moan escape my lips.

My finger tips reached for the keyboard. I tried to remember where I was looking at the broken sentence from earlier. Before Aiden had come in, I was just writing down ideas and had no idea where I was with the actual essay. I deleted the last sentence as he pulled his finger from me and slowly dragged them up to my clit. I typed slowly.

'This conveys that the witches...'

My brain was already mush and Aiden was torturing me.

When my fingers stopped typing, so would Aiden, his hand landing a sharp smack on my ass. I gasped and tried to look over my shoulder. The only glimpse I had was when

Aiden reached for the zip of his jeans. My neck strained and I returned looking at the screen.

"Keep typing, Daphne. Be a good girl for me."

My heart fluttered and my fingers began to type slowly as I tried to string sentences and ideas together. However, my mind was on the sounds that I could hear behind me, his zip and the drop of denim onto the floor.

"Pick up your leg." He tapped my left leg; I lifted my foot and he took off one leg of my leggings and then did the same for my right leg, leaving the bottom half of me bare. Aiden pressed himself up against me and while I couldn't see him, I could feel the pulsing hot cock pressed against my backside as he used his hands to massage my ass, now and again lightly smacking the soft skin.

I'd only had my fill of Nate a few days ago and I was gagging for Aiden. I'd completely lost my mind at this point.

I tried to keep my fingers moving, giving up on typing anything that made sense or was close to my notes. There was no way I'd be able to concentrate. Aiden pulled apart my ass to get a clearer look at my pussy in this position and then took no time in putting the tip of his thick cock into my pussy. I gripped onto the edge of my desk as he slipped deeper into me, biting down on my lip to hide how good he felt inside of me. That was the worst thing because they all felt so good; I couldn't even compare having sex with them to help me pick… Another reason why I was in such a mess.

A harder smack on my ass jolted me against the chair.

"Keep working," he ordered, taking his hands and placing them on my hips. He began taking slow and deep thrusts into me.

I'd almost punctured my lip holding back and decided to let my body do what it needed. I whimpered as he pushed tight against me, deep inside and moaned as he pulled away. I could feel every pulsing vein on him, telling me how thick he was without seeing it. The more he forced me to write my essay as he fucked me slowly, the more I got hang of it and found some sort of pace.

Only Aiden noticed and his thrusts sped up. The chair leg knocked against the desk, making the entire thing rattle. My fingers began slipping from the keys and the amount of red lines on my documents rose.

"Fuck!" I shouted, not being able to concentrate anymore. I gripped the desk again as Aiden went harder into me. I'd be bruised in my core in the morning from being pressed into the back of the chair. I'd be reminded for days. My eyes glanced at the faded love bite that Nate had marked me with that was peaking over my vest top; my tits were barely contained anymore. Aiden pulled me against him with every thrust and the slapping of skin on skin was almost in beat to the music down the hall.

Aiden removed one hand and reached around to touch my clit. He rubbed slow circles into it, unlike his hard and fast thrusts. I was starting to become lightheaded as the pressure in my core knotted and I knew I was about to be thrown over the edge and come undone. I was clenching around Aiden and deep moans came from his throat as he sped up his fingers a little. It only took a few seconds as my body tensed and I was flooded with relief. My lips parted as I let out a broken moan, trying to hold myself up while my arms felt like they were about to crumble.

He could see it and slipped out of me. I could feel wetness leak onto my thighs as he turned me around. Aiden directed me down to the floor with a kiss. I came face to face with what had been inside of me. He was thick and there were veins running the length of him. Looking up at him in an attempt to have some control, I darted out my tongue to taste the tip of him. Aiden took a deep breath and grabbed my hair, keeping me at a distance, as his other hand wrapped around his slippery cock and he began to touch himself at a fast rate. The muscles in his core went taunt and then it was only seconds until squirts of thick cum decorated my face. Luckily, he had missed my eyes.

I looked up at him speechless and satisfied.

Aiden had a thin sheen of sweat on his skin and his breath was unsteady. He reached down to tuck loose hair behind my ears and smiled.

"Have you opened your eyes yet?"

"That I'm completely fucked? Yeah." In so many ways. I rose shakily on my knees.

Aiden reached out to grab my elbows to help me to my feet.

"Clean up and come to the party. Please," he sighed.

"I can't and everything is only more confusing now." I shoved past him and grabbed a packet of wipes in my bathroom. I sat down on my bed and wiped away any traces as Aiden put his jeans back on. He passed me a pair of shorts from my drawer and bent down to help slip them on. I furrowed my brows and he ordered me to lift so he could slip them onto my hips. Aiden took the dirty wipes from my hand and dumped them in the bin by my desk. I stayed silent as he pulled back my duvet and nudged me into bed.

"You're so beautiful," he whispered as I lay down. "Just wish you paid attention to what's going on."

"And what's that?" I mumbled.

"You'll figure it out. Get some sleep; I'll tell them to quieten down."

"No need. I like the white noise," I said and rolled over.

Aiden left a kiss on my head and left the room.

I was even more fucked, figuratively and physically, than before.

chapter thirteen

I woke up surprisingly relaxed as I stretched and yawned. The light was peaking through the sides of my blackout curtains. I stood up and walked over to my desk, checking the time on my phone. It was 11am; the party would have only finished a few hours ago.

Those few peaceful moments after waking up were short lived as my sober interactions with Aiden crept into my mind... my hand was placed on the back of the chair that he had fucked me over. I flipped open my laptop; the document I had been working on was a sea of red lines. I wasn't the greatest speller at the best of times but having your flatmate fuck you and order you to write didn't seem to help.

I ran my fingers through my hair and took a deep breath. Now that I had crossed all three lines, there was no way I could hide forever. I grabbed my leggings and my jacket, pulled them on and tucked my phone away in the pocket.

I had time until everyone woke up so there was no need for the nerves that I felt as I walked down the hallway into the kitchen. Which was a mess.

Paper cups were littered on our floor and the 2000s disco balls were still spinning on the ceiling despite the fact it was daylight. A mixture of pizza boxes and chippy wrappers were on the island, some on the floor. The room wasn't even that big; I never understood how so much mess could be caused by a space that could only fit in fifteen people.

I convinced myself that the best way to say sorry for screwing everyone was to clean up the mess, despite not being at the party. I began with picking up all of the litter that was on the floor and counter. That made everything look instantly better. The few cups that weren't paper I washed up and left to dry on the rack. Then I began wiping down the sides. I was in a world of my own, lost in my thoughts of what I was going to say to them all, planning each talk out in my head ten times over.

I was that deep in my thoughts that I didn't realise Eli had walked into the kitchen. I turned around to throw the bacterial wipes in the bin and jumped out of my skin when I spotted him leaning against the door frame. There were bags under his eyes and his dark blue hair was a mess on top of his head. A glass dangled from his long fingers and the position showed off his lean body. There was an urge to lick my lips as my filthy mind drifted back to the night we had spent together.

"Hey." I offered an awkward smile and turned around to keep cleaning, avoiding eye contact at all costs.

"Hey," he croaked, his throat raspy and deep from just waking up. I heard him behind me grabbing a glass of water. "You didn't have to clean up."

"I know." I glanced over my shoulder and gave another smile, then carried on cleaning.

"You've also been cleaning that spot for the last five minutes. I was watching you."

I dropped the wipe and spun around.

"Yeah, world of my own, sorry," I answered, leaning back on the counter.

"I feel like I haven't since you in forever." The look in Eli's read sadness and that took me back. I expected him to be pissed at me after finding out about Nate.

"I haven't been feeling the best."

"Liar. You've been walking around campus with Madison without a care in the world." He rolled his eyes.

"Eli-" I started but never got to finish.

He placed his glass on the side and before I had a chance to breathe another word, he had me pinned against the counter with a hand either side of me.

"No, let me say this. I don't regret what happened that night with us; it was my idea, I ignited it. I also know that Nate doesn't regret what you guys did together. And Aiden was gone way too long last night to be just checking on you. The only one who seems to be so upset is you."

"Because I'm a slut that's slept with all three of her housemates. And don't even get me started on how judgemental our generation can be; could you imagine Olivia and her bitches finding out. I'm really living up to the whore name." I looked him in the eye, for a split second remembering his lips had been buried against my pussy. "And I don't want this to end in a fight because you three are the most important people in my life and the last couple months living with you guys has been everything I wanted from uni. This only ends in tears. I can't do that and keep you all; if I have to avoid you to keep all three of you, then I will."

"Who said you can't have us all?"

I pressed myself further against the counter, pushing it into my back. But then Eli and I realised Nate was standing in the doorway. He was dressed in a shirt and a pair of shorts, his dirty blond hair swept back off his head but unstyled. I'd seen it enough times and knew that Nate was hungover too.

"Don't be ridiculous," I told him.

"If we're honest with ourselves, how were we all gonna live together for a whole year without anything happening?" Nate walked towards Eli and I, standing beside me. He reached out and tucked a piece of hair behind my ear. "You're stunning, Daph."

"Agreed," Eli spoke.

"I knew what I was getting into when I slept with you; I already knew about you and Eli." Nate swallowed.

"And I knew as soon as you walked about the club together," Eli added.

"And Aiden?" I whispered.

"I already told you he was gone way too long last night." Eli reached for my hand, intertwining our fingers.

"I still don't know how we're meant to move forward," I spoke softly. My heart felt as if it was going to beat out of my chest. What way could I move forward when I had slept with all three of your flatmates and none of them were bothered that I had? Everything I had been worried about seemed pointless all of sudden which only led me to more confusion.

"Like this." Eli grabbed me by the hips and placed me on the island counter. His lips smashed against mine and I was taken back by the sudden kiss. It was the kiss I'd wanted since the night he got rid of my headaches. I kissed back out of muscle memory, my arms reached up to hang over his shoulders. As he deepened the kiss, I wrapped my leg around the back and pushed him closer to me.

When we finally pulled away, I dipped my head and turned towards Nate, waiting for the bust up. Instead Nate grabbed my face and pulled me into his own searing kiss. Eli moved his hands further up my body, reaching my tits. I hadn't put on a bra which gave him perfect access.

I moaned against Nate's lips as Eli rubbed my nipples with his thumbs. I was melting against Nate, having to move my hands to balance myself sitting up. Then Eli pinched both of my hardening nipples and I pulled, gasping. I looked between them both and they looked at each other.

"Nate's one of my closest friends and it's only been a couple of months," Eli explained.

"And Eli is one of mine. We don't expect you to choose. We don't think you *need* to."

"This flat is our bubble. It's the four of us."

"What are you trying to say?"

"They're saying we want to share you. We want you to have all of us." Aiden walked into the kitchen and took his place next to Nate and Eli. My three flatmates stood in front of me, offering to share myself between them and stopping the one thing I had worried about, choosing.

chapter fourteen

"As in I'm with all three of you? At the same time?" I sat up and cleared my throat. "That's what you meant when you told me to open my eyes?" I questioned him.

"What's the problem?" Aiden stepped in between my legs. "Everything that happens in this flat is already like we're together. The only thing that we're adding is fucking you." He smirked.

"I don't want to be passed around." I raised my eyebrow.

Aiden rolled his eyes and reached for the waistband of my leggings. His hand found my bare pussy that he'd had only a handful of hours ago. I watched as Eli whispered to Nate; he nodded and disappeared out of the room.

"We don't want to pass you around," he answered, his fingers finding my clit. "We just want you. To share you.

Love you." His eyes locked onto mine as he began to rub circles. "Together," he whispered, leaning in for a short, quick kiss.

"You're three 18 year old guys; why on earth would you want to share one girl when you could have 10 between yourselves."

"Because they aren't you." Eli reached over Aiden and took my chin to make me look at him. "You clearly don't understand how badly we want you."

"Show me," I swallowed, the last of my common senses leaving me. "Let me see how this works and then I'll decide."

Eli slipped off my jacket and took my arms out as Aiden rubbed my pussy harder. I let out a small whimper, feeling the knot in my stomach, only to have it taken away from me as Aiden stepped back. I looked down at his joggers; he was straining against the grey fabric.

Nate returned to the room, placing something on the stool that I couldn't see.

"We're gonna show her how this works," Aiden told him. "Our girl wants to see what it's gonna be like to be with all three of us."

"Oh Daph, the best time of your fucking life." Nate smirked as Eli placed his lips against my neck, tugging at the waistband of my leggings. I lifted my hips up and Eli managed to pull my leggings from under my ass, taking them off and discarding them to the floor. My bare half was exposed to the three of them. Their eyes trained onto my bare pussy, my legs slightly parted.

Eli dragged his finger up my pussy and smirked when he turned to our friends.

"Already wet."

"Take off her top," Aiden ordered, readjusting himself. Nate leaned on the counter, eyes trained on me. Eli grabbed the hem of my top and I lifted my arms to help him. My nipples were already peaked and hard, my pussy was wet, and all three men were staring at me as if they wanted to devour every inch of me. It somewhat gave me a confidence boost.

Eli dipped down and took one of my nipples into his mouth, one of his hands finding my clit and rubbing. I leant my head back, little moans escaping my mouth when he bit down.

"Put her on the counter, spread her legs," Aiden spoke again. Eli pulled away and did as Aiden asked. I helped, pulling my legs up and laying down on the cold surface that ran a shiver down my spine. Eli spread my legs and I put my knees up, giving Nate and Eli a better view. I looked to the side, Aiden was still against the fridge, palming himself through his joggers. There was a small wet patch on the fabric.

Nate grabbed my ankles, pulling me down the counter further before he placed his mouth onto my clit, his eyes looking up at me as he slowly used his tongue against me. Eli groaned as he re-positioned himself too; he looked at Aiden who had taken the role of the leader in this whole thing.

"You've taken us all but how about together? Think you can handle all three of us?" Aiden asked me.

"Yes," I answered, my breath unsteady.

"That's our good girl," he moaned, finally reaching into his joggers to touch himself as Nate moved further down my pussy to fuck me with his tongue.

"Three holes. Three of us," Eli spoke. "It's perfect." It was clear that my ass was going to be included in whatever we would end up doing. It was something new which made it nerve wracking but also, at the same time, followed the pattern of excitement that came with all three men wanting me.

"I've never done anal," I moaned as Nate gave a hard suck of my clit before he came up for air. His mouth was covered in my pussy.

"That's why we're gonna prepare you, make this good for you. We promise."

"Okay," I whispered. "I trust you."

I was insane. These three guys had all the power in the room and I was laid before them like a meal. I heard a small click sound and lifted myself onto my elbows. Nate stood at the end of the counter with a small bottle of lube. I swallowed. He squirted some onto his fingers and dropped the bottle on the stool. It must have been what he had gone to get earlier.

"This might be a little cold," he warned me.

I hissed at the cold feeling on my ass. Nate rubbed around the tight hole and slowly began working one finger into my ass. Eli stepped forward and stroked my hair before reaching down to touch my clit. The pleasure helped with the stretching.

"How does that feel?" Nate asked.

I nodded, unable to find the ability to form words.

"She nodded. She's okay," Aiden told him. As soon as Nate had the go ahead, he started to add another finger. I reached out to grab the sides of the counter; my bed would have been a lot more comfy than the solid countertop that was no doubt going to ruin my back.

It didn't take long for Nate to have his second finger buried deep inside of me while Eli worked on my clit. The familiar sensation in my core was starting to overwhelm me. Aiden stepped forward and leaned over me, one hand balanced on the counter and the other cup my cheek.

With each one of them touching me in their own way, I had been thrown off the edge. My body shivered as my orgasm ran through every nerve in my body... Aiden's lips on mine, consuming my moans as I came, taking my pleasure for himself. Aiden pulled away, his lips hovering over mine as his eyes locked with my own. A small smile dancing on his lips.

"We need more room," Eli spoke, removing his fingers from my clit as Nate comfortably pushed in another finger.

Three.

I turned my head towards the sofa area; Eli was pulling the various pillows and blankets that were stuffed behind the sofa onto the floor to make it comfier. Then he came over to me on the other side to Aiden, planting soft kisses along my jaw. I turned my head further to meet his lips with a soft kiss.

Nate pulled his fingers out and I moaned at the shiver that ran through my body.

"Three fingers and one orgasm; I think you're ready." Nate kissed my inner thigh. "You wanna choose, sweetheart? Who gets the pleasure of each hole?"

Aiden and Eli helped me sit up, my body still revelling in my orgasm. I swung my legs towards Eli.

"Can you - Can you, you know, anal?" I asked him. Eli's eyes twinkled.

"I got you, baby." He planted a light kiss on my lips.

I looked over my shoulder.

"Just like last night?" I asked Aiden. I liked the way he fucked me with no mercy. Aiden nodded.

I looked at Nate, who was leaning on the counter, watching me.

"And you can be in your favourite place."

"You know it." Nate smiled.

"You still good with this?" Eli asked, gripping my bare hips as I slipped down. Aiden walked around the island as Nate pulled off his shirt. Aiden grabbed my face and forced a devouring kiss onto my already swelling lips as he guided us down to the makeshift bed that Eli had created on the floor.

Aiden pulled me down on top of him; I was straddling him, lost in our kiss. My wet pussy and thighs sitting directly over his grey joggers, his hard-on pressed against me. He let go of my face and moved to tug down the barrier between us. I reached back to help as he kicked off his joggers.

We were naked on top of each other as I rubbed my wet pussy against his cock and made him moan. Eli moved behind me, his lips leaving a small trail down the bottom of my back to my ass. I shivered at the sensation that coursed through my body as I made out with Aiden. Nate kneeled beside me, stroking my hair and naked as well. Aiden was not bothered by the fact that his friend's cock was extremely close to his face.

Eli parted my ass and brushed a finger over my stretched and lubed hole, rubbing his fingers around and teasing me by slipping in two fingers. I pulled away from Aiden, breathless.

"Okay, someone needs to fuck me before I lose my mind," I heaved.

"As you wish," Aiden replied, lifting up my hips and then landing me directly on top of his cock. I gasped as he filled me, wrapping my fingers in the blanket on the floor and throwing my head back. "That's a good girl," he teased, beginning to rock his hips up into me.

"Fuck," I mumbled. Eli touched my ass again, rubbing some extra lube around my tight hole.

"Are you gonna be okay, baby?" he asked, palming my ass. I nodded.

"Yes, yes, I wanna try. I want it." I barely made out.

Eli positioned himself behind me, grasping my ass and slowly pressing his hard cock against my ass, right at the entrance. Aiden stopped thrusting inside of me, just as Eli pushed himself inside of me, through the ring of muscle and that's what hurt the most. Nate, who was waiting at the sidelines, kissed me and lowered his arm to touch my clit to help me through it.

"She's okay," Aiden spoke, Nate's mouth busy with mine. "Keep going. She can take it, I know she can. Such a good girl, aren't you, Daph?"

The praise sent butterflies through my stomach and I moaned against Nate as Eli pushed himself further inside of me.

I could feel them both inside of me, Aiden and Eli brushing against one another. That's how big they were, it felt as if they were pressed together.

"Almost there, baby." Eli squeezed my ass. "Fuck, you're so fucking tight. Shit." He cursed and then he bottomed out inside of me, pressed against my ass.

Nate pulled away from me and looked over at my bottom half where two cocks were filling me up and that was enough for Nate to pull out his cock from his shorts and touch himself.

"Ready?" Aiden asked under me. I nodded. Aiden slowly pulled out of me and, like a well oiled machine, he pushed back inside of me as Eli pulled out. They were slow at first, working in tandem until they found a rhythm. My lips parted as I was fucked, the pleasure pooling in my stomach. I held it back; I wanted this feeling to last. Be on the edge of pleasure for as long as I could be.

Nate took advantage of my parted lips, grabbing my face and turning it towards him. He pushed his cock between my lips and I ran my tongue under the head to watch his eyes light up. One hand reached for my messy hair, wrapping it in his fist as he held me in place, bobbing his cock into my mouth as our friends fucked my ass and pussy.

The pace quickened, Eli pulled out, Aiden pushed in, Eli pushed in and Aiden pulled out. My mouth was full of Nates cock; he had started to fuck me at the same speed that my holes were being wrecked. The only sounds in the room were the slapping of skin and me sucking on Nate as he pushed my gag reflex to the limit. All that my brain could process was the pleasure in my core. I clenched around them and Aiden reached to dig his fingers into my hips. Focusing what brain power I had left, I carried on sucking Nate's cock; I hollowed my cheeks and used my tongue against the veins on the sensitive skin. Nate threw his head back.

"Fucking hell, sweetheart. I could have your lips wrapped around my cock all day long."

I moaned against him in response as Aiden and Nate changed their rhythm. They pushed inside of me at the same time and I pulled away from Nate's cock to scream out.

"Fuck!" I swore as they sped up, stretching me in ways that I didn't think were possible. Nate didn't appreciate his cock being left out and pushed himself back into my mouth. I made eye contact with him as I sucked harder. His eyes almost rolled into the back of his head.

"Oh sweetheart, I'm about to fill that dirty mouth of yours if you don't stop," he warned me.

I closed my eyes and concentrated on sucking the sensitive swollen head.

"Fuck," he growled and pushed his entire cock down my throat. I gagged and breathed through my nose. Seconds later, hot warm cum shot down my throat. Once he filled my mouth and slowly pulled out, he had left his mark on my tongue. I tried my best to swallow everything but some escaped the corner of my lips. Aiden watched.

"That's the hottest thing I've ever seen. You being so full of us," he mumbled. "Gonna fill you up, our good girl." With one last sharp thrust, Aiden pushed inside of me and left his own mark. His cum filled my pussy just like it had last night and it threw me over the edge.

Clenching around him as I milked him for everything he had, I came again. My body felt as if it were floating as Aiden slipped out of me. Nate sat back watching as Eli fucked my ass.

Aiden shuffled from under me and placed my hands on the floor; I was on all fours as Eli fucked my ass. He was rougher than he had been the first time. He reached forward, grabbing a fist full of my hair and pulling it back as he thrusted inside of me.

"One more, come on baby, come with me."

I'd have no problem following Eli's orders as I could already feel my third orgasm in my core building with every thrust of my ass as Aiden's cum dripped out of me and onto the blanket below.

"I'm close," I moaned, balancing on one hand to gather some of the leaked cum from Aiden and using it to rub circles around my clit. I could still taste the saltiness in my mouth from Nate. Even if they had finished, it felt like they were still fucking me too.

"Come on baby, finish for me," he begged and I could tell he was on the edge.

"I'm gonna come!" I screamed out and Eli did three last sharp and deep thrusts into my ruined ass. I came, another gush between my legs as I felt the new sensation of being filled in the ass.

When he was finished, Eli pulled out, parting my ass to watch his handy work. I pulled away and lay down on the ground, my breathing unsteady and sweaty. Aiden lay next to me, Nate on my other side and Eli squeezed himself in to rest his head on my hip. I ran my fingers through his hair.

Aiden did the same to me as Nate traced a pattern on my messy thighs. I could feel everything leaking out of me and licked my lips to taste Nate.

"Are you okay?" Aiden whispered to me.

I nodded. "I'm perfect. I feel like I'm on cloud nine," I sighed.

"So you liked it?" Nate asked.

"Yeah." I smiled at him. "Do you really think it could work?" I asked them.

"We'll only know if we try and I think I speak for all of us when I say we want to." Eli looked up at me. "Still, I think I'm surprised at how this has all turned out."

"You guys really think you can share and not make me crazy with all your caveman attitude?"

"I think we share pretty well, don't you?" Aiden spoke.

"Yeah but what if sometimes I'm only with one of you?"

"Us three can figure that out. You don't need to worry," Nate answered.

"Okay. We can try," I spoke, closing my eyes, completely worn out.

"Hey, don't fall asleep yet." Eli nudged me. "Let's get you cleaned up first."

I nodded, half asleep, as the boys pulled away from me. Eli held out his hand and helped me to my feet.

"Maybe we should look for a place with a bath for the second year," Nate said, grabbing his shorts from the floor.

"Hmm, I like that," I mumbled. "Cause I need some serious relaxing after that." I joked as Eli grabbed Nate's shirt for me to wear.

"Go get yourself ready for round two, sweetheart."

I rolled my eyes at Nate's comment and walked out the room while Eli held me up.

chapter fifteen

THE BOYS LEFT ME alone to shower and get myself sorted. Once I was in a fresh and soft tracksuit to look after my sore muscles, I went back into the kitchen.

I was surprised that all three of them were chilling in their boxers and yet I was the one who felt naked. I pulled my sleeves down. They didn't notice me straight away so I took a moment to admire them, putting my head against the door frame with a smile on my face. The anxiety that had flooded my mind when I had woken up was gone and I was left with pure bliss.

It didn't take long for Aiden to notice me and gently pat the spot next to him on the sofa. I stepped over Nate's legs where he was sitting against the wall. Curling up on the sofa beside Aiden, I tucked my legs underneath myself and leaned against his warm skin.

Aiden took the opportunity to steal a kiss and I blushed, looking away. Kissing in front of the other two, whoever it was with, was going to take some getting used to.

"How are you feeling, baby?" Eli called over to me from the other sofa.

"Tired but....peaceful," I answered.

"So, can we really make this work?" Nate asked. "I mean, that was good," he swallowed. "I didn't expect that but it was the best thing I've ever experienced."

"I mean, you suggested it first," I reminded him.

"Actually, that was Aiden." Eli nodded towards him. "Although, I didn't know he was in the running. You're a dark horse." He chuckled as I looked up at Aiden.

"Really?"

"I gave them the nudge, wanted to see your reaction with the two of them before I stepped in."

"It's what we were talking about that night you saw us."

It made sense why they had stopped talking when I had walked into the room now. They had been talking about *me*, maybe even thinking of the insane idea that the four of us should be together.

"So, you know my older sister? Lola?" Aiden spoke, wrapping his arm around me.

"Yeah, of course." I nodded.

"She reads, way too much in my opinion, but there are these books she likes. They have a trope or something called reverse harem where a girl ends up with multiple boys. She falls for them all, ends up loving them. We all worked so well together; most of the flats have fallen out by now and we haven't. It made sense. And when I caught you sneaking out of Nate's room, it crossed my mind." Aiden was blushing.

The look in those boyish green eyes told me that he had really considered it. He'd thought about the way our home worked the same way I had. The internal fight began again that I couldn't have them all but I wanted it all. I wanted *them*.

I leaned up and stole my own kiss.

"Hey, that's two now," Eli teased. "Aren't we all meant to be equal?"

"Come here and I'll give you a kiss, mate." Nate puckered his lips. "I'm kidding, that I *can't* handle. Promise me we are not doing that?" He looked around at us all, panicked and startled like a caught deer about the thought of having to kiss one of his best friends.

All four of us laughed. Nate crawled across the small space and then placed his hands on the sofa, lifting himself to press a sweet and longing kiss against my lips which I gladly returned. He pulled away and sat against the sofa. Eli joined him on the floor, sitting close enough that he could trace light patterns on my calf.

"What if it doesn't work?" I whispered. "Everyone is already starting to think about housing for next year. What if we decide we want to live together again but it all goes wrong and we're trapped?"

"I promise, and I'm sure Nate and Aiden agree, that you'll never be trapped. If we find somewhere and you decide you need out, then we'll pay you back any deposit and you're free to go wherever you want to." Eli kissed my knees. "You're our girlfriend now and we care about your happiness."

"For now, let's take it one step at a time," Aiden spoke.

"But if you feel like you need space or it's too much, then you need to promise that you'll talk to us. The same goes for us guys too. I think it's important that we all communicate."

"Yeah, I agree." Eli nodded.

"Me too."

"Deal." I grinned, looking around at my... boyfriends. "I liked us all being together. But for now, can we just stay inside of our bubble? Keep it to ourselves? I've already been called a slut by Olivia and her bitches."

"Just us." Aiden kissed the top of my head.

"And I don't want them around anymore," I spoke up, sitting up straight. "We need to remember to lock the door. Especially now you're my...boyfriends."

Eli left to his feet and went into the kitchen area, rummaging around in the drawers. The three of us watched him as he found some sticky notes and a sharpie. He pulled the lid off and put it in his mouth while scrawling something down. When he was done, he lifted it to show us.

DND.

"What does that mean?" I asked.

"Do not disturb," Nate answered.

"And it's going straight on the front door," Eli said. He headed for the front door.

"Eli, you're in boxers!" I called out, rolling my eyes and laughing at him.

"Shit." He dipped inside the kitchen again and looked around for his bottoms. Once they were back on, he went to put the sign on the door.

"So, you're okay?" Aiden asked.

"More than okay. I'm the happiest girl in the world."

eight months later

How do you make it work with 3 boyfriends? Not that anyone has ever asked me that. We'd kept our relationship under wraps for the past 8 months, wanting to decide if it was the right choice before dealing with how we'd explain it all to everyone. We were happy in our bubble and somehow it worked.

I had a relationship with each of them and then we had one together. Sometimes I'd spend the night in one of their rooms and other times we dragged mattresses into the living room to all be together. Eli, Nate, and Aiden each took me out on dates, although 9 times out of 10 it would end up the 4 of us. The jealousy I'd expected to see was non-existent.

In the New Year, we'd decided to take a leap of faith and sign up for our second-year house together. It was an easier decision when we already lived together but we still had to consider that if things didn't work out, everything would be ruined between us .

Thankfully, things had gone well and we were all staying in our new home together throughout the summer. We'd managed to cram everything in Aiden's seriously small car that he'd brought back from home. It took at least ten trips to get everything we all owned in the new house. Layers of sweat were on all of us and, as the sun set in our new back garden, I laid in the bath, using a towel as a pillow and sighing.

"You okay, baby?"

I opened one eye and saw Eli unpacking his toiletries on the unit in the bathroom.

"Yeah, just worn out." I smiled, turning my head to watch him.

"Well, Aiden is going to get dinner and then we can all chill in the back garden, have a few drinks."

"Plan your year of partying more like," I teased.

Eli walked over and kneeled beside the bath, stroking my hair back.

"I love you, Daph," he whispered.

"I love you too." I took some bubbles onto my finger and wiped them onto his nose. Eli reached out to tease my nipples that were poking out of the bath and I squirmed. Having three boyfriends had increased my sex drive and I was ready to go at any time and anywhere.

"Eli!" I warned. He squeezed my nipple and I groaned.

"Starting tomorrow, I plan to eat you out on the dining table daily," he leaned over to whisper in my ear. After a quick nip to my earlobe, he released my nipple and swapped it for a consuming kiss that nearly had me sinking into the water. "Bye, baby. Don't take too long." He stood up and left me alone in our large new bathroom.

Once I had got dressed and unpacked some of my clothes, Aiden was calling for me that dinner was ready.

The hallway was narrow with a beautiful red front door. When you walked in, there was a living room on the right, the stairs in front to the left. Further down the corridor, there was one of the bedrooms, the one that Aiden had claimed. Then straight ahead was the kitchen-diner, also on the smaller side, but I had no doubt the boys would pack it full for their parties. It was also where the back door was.

I stepped out into the garden and followed the path to the patio. Nate was hanging fairy lights on the back wall. Eli was sitting on the camping chairs with a little BBQ that was being used as a fire pit. Aiden sat on another chair, opening the carrier bag with our chippy inside.

I sat down on one of the chairs as Aiden handed me my food.

"Thank you." I began to unwrap my dinner. Aiden made sure my battered sausage and chips were separate; just the way I liked it. I dumped the extra paper on the ground and put my food on my lap.

Aiden passed me a tub of curry sauce, pressing a quick kiss to my lips. After Nate finished with the fairy lights he kissed my cheek as he took the final seat around the fire. I smiled, looking around at my guys.

Being out of the flat block was a completely different atmosphere. There was no constant noise. The street was quiet and peaceful. It almost felt like home even after one day.

"I could get used to this," I spoke, popping a chip into my mouth.

Only peace never lasted.

The back door of the house next to ours opened. I looked over my shoulder at the wall separating the gardens.

And then there she was.

Olivia.

Peeping over the garden wall.

"Well, imagine seeing you guys here." She smirked. "Looks like we're neighbours again."

I turned my back to her.

Just my fucking luck.

acknowledgements

Thank you to everyone who has read my books, and I hope you love this hardback edition. First of all, a big shout out to my author besties, Emma and Faith, for their support in the past year, I would not have reached this point without you and probably retreated back into my cave.

Al, I say this all the time but thank you for being my best friend through thick and thin. You've been around since I first started publishing and one of my greatest cheerleaders since day one. Not only that but thanks to you I met T.

T Cake, my hype woman, I will never forget you sitting on my sofa with your highlighter proof reading for me. I'm so lucky to have you in my life.

about the author

Em Solstice is a romance author from the UK. As well as procrastinating writing fast-paced novellas with a spicy twist, she enjoys snuggling her cat and drinking Starbucks... and waiting for her own love story to begin.